SUFFOLK GHOST TALES

Suffolk Ghost Tales

Kirsty Hartsiotis &
Cherry Wilkinson

To Heather,
daughter of Suffolk and
sharer of tales.

First published 2017

The History Press
The Mill, Brimscombe Port
Stroud, Gloucestershire, GL5 2QG
www.thehistorypress.co.uk

British Library Cataloguing in Publication Data.
A catalogue record for this book is available from the British Library.

ISBN 978 0 7509 7009 9

Typesetting and origination by The History Press
Printed and bound in Great Britain by TJ International Ltd, Padstow, Cornwall

Contents

Acknowledgements 7

Map of the Stories 8

Illustrations 9

Introduction 10

1 The Haunting of William Hurr 13

2 Toby, the Black Dragoon 19

3 The Treasure Seeker 26

4 These Lovers Fled Away 32

5 The Rougham Mirage 38

6 The Lowestoft Witches 44

7 The Constant Maid 51

8 The Secret Burial 57

9 A Gift from the Sea 64

10 The Mistletoe Bride 69

11 If You Go into the Woods 75

12 Mrs Henrietta Nelson is at Home 81

13 The Suffolk Rising 87

14 The Chiming Hours 94

15 The Ghosts of Landguard Fort 99

16 Lady in Grey 105

17	Monks of the Buttermarket	110
18	The Murderess's Daughter	116
19	Newmarket Legends	122
20	The Mill Cat	127
21	Kate's Parlour	133
22	The *Mayfly*	140
23	The Educating of Ellen de Freston	148
24	The Haunting of Old Hall	154
25	The Unlayable Ghost	160
26	The Vagabond Nun	166
27	The Luck of Hintlesham	173
28	Witch and Rabbit	178
29	The Honington Ghost	183
30	The Afterlife of St Edmund	191
	Bibliography	199
	Index	202
	About the Authors	205

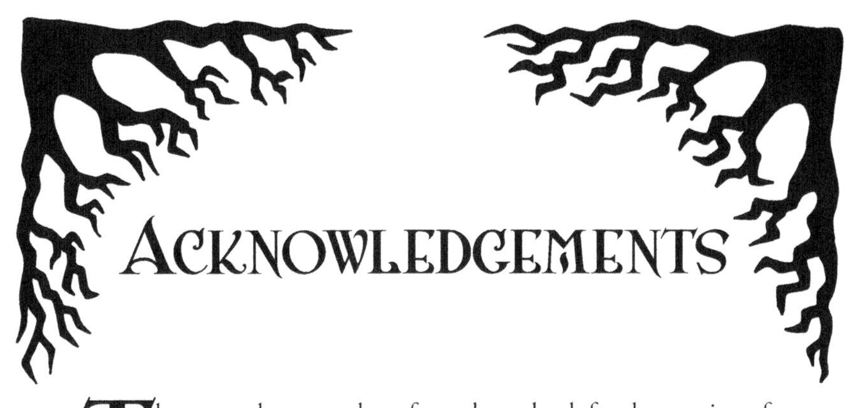

Acknowledgements

There are a large number of people to thank for the creation of this book. Many people have assisted with the stories: special thanks go to Heather Phillips MBE for the loan of books, use of stories from her mother's memoirs, personal recollections and her extensive local knowledge. Thanks go to Boni Sones OBE and Alan Warne for their memories of Sizewell, and to Boni for access to her film, *A Dream for Sizewell.* Thank you to Majorie Onyett for her story. We'd also like to thank Gabby Ballantine, Cyrilla Havard, Dr Simon Heywood, Dr Katherine Lewis, Sally MacDonald, Dr Victoria Thompson and Rev. Anna Wright for the loan of books, help with Bible texts, assistance with research, location information and Latin translation. We'd also like to thank the Norfolk Wherry Trust's *Albion* volunteers, Pegasus Stables, Newmarket, Hintlesham Hall's front of house team, and the owners of Yaxley Hall for the personal tours we received and the questions answered.

Thanks also are due to Ruth Boyd, Laura Kinnear, Chantelle Smith and Kevan Manwaring for listening to and commenting on the tales, as well as the members of Stroud Out Loud and Newent Storytelling, who have also heard many tales.

The greatest thanks go to our partners, without whose support we couldn't have written the book you see today. They walked (and drove!) with us on our ghostly journey. Firstly, to Anthony Nanson, who listened to and discussed stories, visited many sites with us, and, most critically, freely gave his considerable editing expertise and copy-editing skills to help us make this book the very best it could be. Secondly, to David Wilkinson for his local knowledge, contacts, assistance with research and for driving us all over the county … and also for the luminescent shrimps.

MAP OF THE STORIES

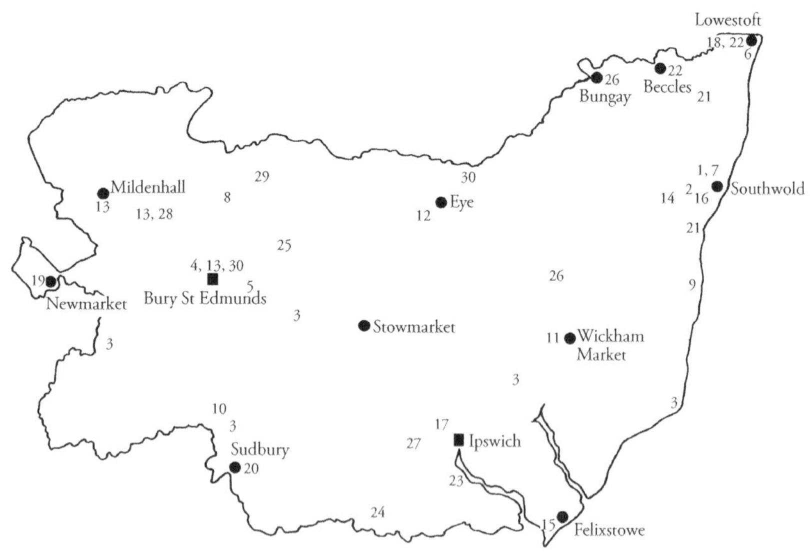

Illustrations

The cover illustration is by Katherine Soutar and illustrates 'The Treasure Seeker'. The map and illustrations within each story are by Kirsty Hartsiotis (© 2017). All other illustrations are from the Dover Pictorial Archive and are reproduced in accordance with their terms and conditions.

Introduction

Suffolk must be one of the spookiest counties in Britain. It was the childhood home of one of Britain's best-loved writers of ghost stories, M.R. James. Suffolk's long shingle beaches, its small stately homes, its ancient monuments, its woods and its marshes inspired his tales. And lurking in the woods, the seaside villages and in towns are hundreds of ghosts. Those hanged for murder haunt the place of their gibbeting. Grey ladies drift, disconsolate, in manor houses. Ghosts rise from lonely ponds, flit through town-centre car parks, wreak havoc on people's property and promise riches that disappear in the light of day.

Most ghost sightings are as ephemeral as the spectres themselves, so we have worked these tales into fully dramatised stories that we hope will be retold again and again. We've tried to include many different kinds of ghost, from poltergeists, to imprints of calamitous events, to the traditional ghost who retains his or her personality – as well as a selection of animal spirits. Ultimately, though, the tales we chose are the ones that most caught our imagination. This volume of thirty stories is a companion to Kirsty's *Suffolk Folk Tales*, so we've avoided repeating the seven ghost stories included in that book: 'The Rat Pipers of Beccles', 'The Suffolk Miracle', 'The Guardian of the Breckland', 'The Murder in the Red Barn', 'Maude Carew', 'The Dauntless Girl' and 'The Ghost Who Cared Too Much'.

One thing we've been struck by is how personal ghost stories are. Unlike many folk tales, where the protagonist is an archetype – a princess, a fool, a third son – ghost tales are usually the stories of real people. Sometimes, the known person is the one recounting the sighting of the ghost. Often, the ghost is a historical personage whose story you can look up in contemporary records, such as Blythburgh's drummer Toby, or Lowestoft's Amy Denny and Rose Cullender. On occasion, the ghost's personal story has faded away, but the history of the place can shed light on the haunting. We've dug down as deep as we can into these histories to recreate our own versions of their tales.

Unlike with fairies, giants or dragons, many people still believe in ghosts and have had their own experiences. One chilling tale recounted to us in the course of researching the book came from a neighbour of Cherry's. During the Second World War, she was working as a land girl near the Saints. Cycling back to the farm one evening after visiting her family in Reydon, she saw ahead of her a figure dressed in a long robe, with long hair that seemed to glow. Unnerved, she pedalled faster to overtake him. It seemed to take forever to get past and, as she drew level, she heard the sound of horses, though there were none nearby. When she finally passed him, she looked back – and no one was there! It isn't for us to decide what the truth behind these tales is. This was our informant's lived experience. Just like all those who've recorded sightings of ghosts over the centuries, all the way back to the chronicler of the ghost of Leofstan in the twelfth century, those who've seen and heard of such things have made up their own minds about what happened. And, as you read and enjoy our tales, so must you.

Kirsty Hartsiotis and Cherry Wilkinson

1

The Haunting of William Hurr

William Hurr was a master mariner, captain of his own ship these many years, trading back and forth across the North Sea. In 1793 he was fifty-six years old and starting to think about retiring. His Mary had been on at him to come home to Southwold ever since the Frenchies decided to up and overthrow their king. Hurr knew in his heart of hearts that she was right, especially after the news came that they'd killed old Louis, but he had goods ready and waiting to go. One more trip wouldn't hurt. Then he'd stay home for good.

Hurr was wrong. In the time it took him to reach Calais, France had declared war on Britain. As soon as they reached the port, there were soldiers all over the boat; his goods were confiscated and his ship impounded.

'That ship will be serving la République now!' he was told, then he and his men were marched away.

It was the last he would see of his crew for some time. The men were taken away to barracks with barely more than the clothes they stood up in. Hurr got a clip on the ear for begging they be given their wages. He was told to keep his money to himself – he'd be needing it.

He was lodged first in a house in Calais with other merchant officers, a mix of disgruntled Brits and Dutchmen. The only men who remained with him were his first mate, Sam May, and May's brother Jim, the second mate. Hurr spoke both French and Dutch, but it was hard, locked up and having to spend their money to pay for bed and board. He wrote to Mary, but was too proud to beg for money to pay for his release.

After a time the French moved them inland. Hurr was restless without the sound of the sea and the bustle of the port.

He muttered to the Mays, 'Do they think we're fool enough to stow away on a warship back home?'

The first couple of months they were moved again and again. If Mary replied, her letter was lost somewhere in Picardy. Eventually they ended up in Dieppe. The sailors, English and Dutch alike, relaxed when they heard the gulls and smelt the tang of the sea. But it was still captivity. The months went by and funds were wearing thin. The sailors set to carving and whittling, making model ships and pipes to pay for their vittles.

Having a place to rest your head and enough to eat only goes so far in satisfying a man's needs. They whiled away the time with cards and dice, but that wasn't all. At first the locals had steered clear of the foreigners, but after a while some of the women, realising the commercial opportunities, started to visit, selling food – and other things.

There was one woman who caught Hurr's eye. Her name was Genevieve. As her visits became more frequent, he realised she was as taken with him as he was with her. She was a fine woman: dark hair, dark eyes and a fiery tongue. She was no slip of lass, being a widow in her thirties, but to Hurr she was perfection.

The only problem was Mary back in Southwold.

'You have to tell her you're a married man, Will,' Sam May told him.

'It's not fair on Mary, and it's not fair on the lass,' said Jim. 'We've seen how she looks at you. She's thinking you're a keeper, and no mistake.'

But Hurr said nothing, even though Genevieve often spoke of a future for them together. He let her draw her own conclusions. If she thought him widowed, where was the harm in this foreign land?

The months turned into a year, then two. Even as he carried on with Genevieve, Hurr was writing home to Mary, asking for money now, for his release. He wasn't proud of it, but a man couldn't be a captive all his life. Eventually the money came, with sad words from his son: Mary was ill; would he please hurry home?

When he told Genevieve he was going home, she was thrilled.

'We can start a new life back in your Southwold, Guillaume. You can fish, and I will keep house for you.'

Now he wished he'd taken the Mays' advice. He told her that he was still married, that he had been married to Mary for thirty years and more. He stoically withstood the shouting and screaming that followed, knowing he well deserved it. But Genevieve was made of sterner stuff than he'd thought.

When he explained his wife was ill, her lips thinned and she said, 'Guillaume, this is how it shall be. If your wife she is dead when you return, you will write to me and I will come. And if she is not – well, I am young, I will wait.'

Hurr had to smile. She was magnificent! Cravenly, he agreed.

When Hurr got home to Southwold, Mary was alive and, if not well, clearly getting better. Genevieve had to be put from his mind. He bought shares in his son's fishing boat and began to rebuild his life.

After a month or so of his being home, a strange thing happened. Mary began to complain that he was poking and pinching her in bed. After two long years of forced inactivity and now enduring the long, hard hours of a fisherman, Hurr had no energy to do anything in bed except sleep.

'Then who is poking me?' cried Mary.

Hurr shrugged, assuming whatever was troubling her would stop soon enough. But it didn't. Every time Mary woke him to tell him to stop, he'd been sound asleep. He protested his innocence every time, but she'd just shake her head and mutter that some things had been easier when he was away.

Then, one night, he saw it happen. In the moonlight slanting through the window, Mary's face suddenly snapped from side to side, as if someone was slapping her. She began to writhe about and, to his horror, he saw the skin go in on her face as if someone was poking her. Through this Mary slept, but then she was suddenly jerked upwards and her eyes flew open in terror. He reached for her, but before he could grab her she was pitched right out of bed.

Hurr couldn't understand it, but what soon became clear was that it only happened when he was there. Lying on a pallet by the fire in the kitchen he'd examine his conscience and, though he tried not to, remember Genevieve's soft embrace. Was his own dissatisfaction causing the strange thing that had been happening?

One night, his old bones were aching too much for him to get to sleep on his pallet, so up he got in his nightshirt and went outside, brooding out over South Green to the sea. It was full moon, and he stood there a while, thinking on the past.

Suddenly, a white cat appeared not twenty paces before him on the Green. Cats move fast, but it was as if it had been conjured from the moonlight. And no ordinary cat, this – it was as big as a dog! Hurr rubbed his eyes, thinking the moonlight had tricked him, but no, there it was, larger than life, staring at him with eyes that seemed to bore into his soul. As he stared back, Hurr realised that not only was the cat huge, but it was glowing, as if it were part moonlight itself.

'Whsst!' he cried.

The cat just stared.

Hurr grabbed his stick and ran at it, crying, 'Get out, cat!'

Any normal cat would have leapt away, but this one held its ground, hissing and arching its back. Then, it reared up, getting bigger and bigger till a huge white shadow loomed over him and he fell to his knees in terror. The cat was gone, but in its place was a glowing white mare with steam pooling from her nostrils.

For a long time, horse and man stared at each other, then, with a swish of her tail, she turned away towards the town. As soon as she was gone, Hurr felt a tugging in his chest. He found himself scrambling to his feet and, in his stockinged feet, following her as if in a dream. It was as if an invisible cord was pulling him after her but he never caught up. As they came on to Queen Street he realised her hooves made no sound on the cobbles. It was late, no lights anywhere save for the moon, but she illuminated the street with every step.

She led him to Market Place, then, with a lift of her head as if she sensed something, she vanished. The invisible cord snapped and Hurr stumbled to a halt. For a few moments, he was able to wonder what was going on.

Then, coming up East Street, as if from the sea, he saw a funeral procession. At the front a solemn-faced priest marched, the mourners in their broad-brimmed hats behind, carrying flickering candelabras, silent men carrying the funeral bier, all draped and plumed in black, and weeping people behind. In Hurr's heart there rose a terrible grief. As the procession passed him by and turned up Church Street, he felt that tug in his chest again, and his feet followed after them in the echoing silence.

St Edmund's rose up, white-roofed in the moonlight, windows dark and empty. The mourners stepped through the gates into the churchyard, but as Hurr followed, the procession vanished. He stood shivering in his dew-soaked stockings for a long time, trying to make sense of what had happened. The longer he stood there, the more unreal it all became.

The next day Hurr rose early and went down to the beach where his boat was moored. Before he'd done a thing, Sam May, who'd been released shortly after him, came over with a very serious expression on his face and a letter in his hand.

'It's from France,' he said.

Afterwards, Hurr would say he knew before he broke the seal. It was from Genevieve's family – sent to May, they explained, lest Hurr's wife saw it. Genevieve hadn't waited to hear from Hurr, they said. She had told them her heart demanded that she see him again, and, wife or no wife, she was determined to have him. Almost as soon as Hurr had left she too had taken sail. But there was a storm, her ship was wrecked and all souls on it were lost.

As he stood with the letter in his hand and the tears tracking down his face, Hurr knew whose unhappy spirit had troubled his wife, and his heart bled for them all.

After the letter came, Mary was able to rest easy in her bed, almost as if Genevieve was content that he knew she was dead. But Hurr knew he had done both his wife and his lover wrong, and feared he would have to atone for his misdeeds.

In 1799 Mary died. She'd not been truly well since before Hurr came home, but he couldn't help wonder whether the haunting had hurried her end.

He took to walking the beach at night, poultering, searching for anything useful washed in by storm and tide. One night, when he was up by the Field Stile, he heard the shingle rattling and looked up to see someone walking towards him. From the line of his clothes in the moonlight, he could see it was no old fisherman like himself, but a gentleman in a tailcoat and britches. The hairs on the back of his neck stood up. Why would a gentleman be out here on a cold night like this, so far from the town?

Sure the man had seen him, Hurr stopped and leant on his stick. Poultering wasn't illegal, but you'd not want to be caught doing it by the gentry. The man stopped when he was within spitting distance. In the moonlight Hurr saw that his face was cruel and cold.

He said, 'Come along with me.'

All at once Hurr felt that strange tugging in his chest, and his eyes went wide. He had no desire to come along with this man! He looked down at the ground and, as he did, saw that the man's feet were not feet at all, but cloven hooves.

With a shock he realised that the Devil himself had come to collect him for payment for his wrongs. Well, he wasn't having it!

'No, I shall not go with you,' he cried. 'By the help of God I have got so far, and by the help of God I hope to get home.'

At the name of God, the figure gave a shrieking cry and a plume of fire and smoke arose around him, swallowing him whole. Hurr was enveloped in the stink of rotten eggs, as if the maw of hell had opened – and perhaps it had.

He walked back slowly to his house. It was empty, as it always was since Mary had gone. He sank into his chair and prodded the fire into life. He'd had a lucky escape there, he thought, but then he looked around the empty room and his shoulders slumped. Escape? Maybe he was being punished after all, with neither of the women he'd loved here to put warmth in his life.

2

Toby, the Black Dragoon

The Reverend Ralph Blois stood in the nave of Blythburgh church and sighed. The church, like the village, was in a sorry state in that year of Our Lord 1750. Ralph's family, the landowners, did what they could, but they couldn't maintain the church as they wished. Ralph held the living of Walberswick as well, and there the people had built a new little church in the ruins of the old.

'The Lord will provide,' he said to himself.

The villagers, he knew, had more pragmatic ways of providing for themselves. The running of contraband had become quite an industry all along the Suffolk coast. Ralph chose to turn a blind eye, since it helped keep bellies full. His silence was rewarded every now and then with a keg of brandy tucked inside the vestry.

So, when a detachment of dragoons arrived in Blythburgh charged with suppressing the smuggling trade, Ralph was as unhappy as the villagers. He knew the dragoons' commander, Sir Robert Rich, a Beccles man, and didn't much care for him. He had a reputation for mistreating his men. He wasn't around a great deal, but this was a mixed blessing, for the soldiers were an unruly bunch.

Under the pretext of spying on the smugglers, they spent a lot of time in the inns and alehouses, bragging about their exploits in Holland and bemoaning the injustice of being sent to such a backwater. Ralph witnessed a fight or two and had to intervene when tankards and tempers overspilled. The villagers hated the dragoons, but he heard stories of battles, fear and loss from those soldiers who had sought him out.

'Perhaps they deserve a little respite,' he thought. 'If only they would behave!'

The village was in uproar after a bevy of dragoons spent hours knocking on doors, searching houses, calling out blasphemies, and all the while that black lad, Toby, rat-a-tat-tatting on his drum.

The villagers didn't dare speak out, but Ralph heard their mutterings.

'Our women aren't safe on the streets!' they'd bluster.

But some whispered, 'A drunken dragoon can't interfere with our business, if you see what I mean.'

Ralph's thoughts were drawn back to the drummer. The young man's skin was black as night. Not a common sight in rural Suffolk! Black drummers were not unusual in the army, but here he stuck out like a sore thumb. 'Is he the Devil?' some of the villages asked in their ignorance.

Toby certainly had a devilish streak. Sober, he was all smiles and charm. The village men muttered about the things the women liked to say about him! But once in the tavern, with a tankard or two of ale inside him, he'd swear and brawl like the rest of them.

Soon, the rowdiest of the dragoons, Toby included, were barred from the local hostelries. But there were plenty of folks ready to sell them liquor. The dragoons would often meet at a lonely barn on the heathland sheep walks between Blythburgh and Walberswick.

Ralph sighed again and sank wearily to his knees to pray.

Moments later, the church door crashed open and two village men burst in.

'Mr Blois, you in here? Come you quick, sir! Summat bad has happened!'

Outside in the street a crowd was gathering. In their midst was a group of men dragging the stumbling figure of Toby. Other men were carrying a makeshift stretcher on which lay a shrouded form. Ralph called for quiet – and an explanation. After some jostling, shepherd Dick Bullen was pushed forward.

'We found them on the walks, sir, early this morning. Thought they were asleep till the lassie couldn't be roused. Dead, sir, and this one here' – he jabbed his finger at Toby – 'dead drunk. Swore he didn't know what'd happened. A likely story, if you ask me!'

Ralph went to the stretcher and lifted the cloth. The young woman's face was waxen in death. For a second he didn't know her, but then he realised. 'Annie Blakemore from Walberswick. I must go to her family.'

Toby was secured in Blythburgh Gaol to await the coroner's inquest. The villagers' feelings were at fever pitch, even before the coroner arrived.

'We knew something like this would happen!' they cried. 'Hang him! Hang the lot of them!'

As soon as he could, Ralph visited Toby in the gaol, and found him in great distress, protesting his innocence.

'I swear I never laid a hand on her, sir. She just appeared out of nowhere and fell at my feet.'

'You were drunk, Toby,' said Ralph. 'How can you know what you did?'

'I just know,' said Toby, his head in his hands. 'But I really was very drunk ...'

Ralph pondered Toby's words. He knew a little more than many about Anne. Her family were as sure as the rest that Toby had murdered her, but Ralph recalled that on occasion they'd thought the girl possessed. Would that not explain the fits she suffered, her restlessness, her constant wandering on the heath? They'd begged him to exorcise her demons, but Ralph was sure that it was some ailment that troubled her, not possession.

Could Toby's protestations be the truth? Or had he succumbed to violence?

Ralph hoped the coroner's inquest would prove things one way or the other. He decided he would speak of Anne's condition only if there was no evidence she'd been attacked. He'd known Coroner Ward for years and trusted him to conduct a fair hearing.

On the eve of the inquest, urgent family business called Ralph away. In his absence the jury of local men pronounced Toby guilty of murder and on 30 June, before Ralph could return, Toby was taken to Ipswich Gaol to await trial at the Bury Assizes.

Ralph had to assume that justice had been done and Toby was a murderer. But doubt niggled at his mind.

At Anne's funeral service in Walberswick, the people of Blythburgh joined their neighbours in mourning. It was an angry day, and the ill feeling towards Toby – and the dragoons – grew stronger as the summer wore on and the date of the trial drew near.

On 25 August a contingent from Blythburgh was at Bury, Ralph included. Toby was charged not only with murder but with rape and defilement. Ralph repeated Toby's plea of innocence, but it was hardly heard in the slew of evidence against him.

'She was murdered,' cried one.

'Strangled,' cried another.

'He's no better than an animal!' shouted a third.

Ralph didn't mention Anne's condition, not wishing to blacken her name when there was so obviously no need.

The judge did not waste time: the verdict was guilty on all counts. Toby would be hanged at Ipswich and his body hung in chains on a gibbet at Blythburgh.

'If I had the power,' declared the judge, 'to extend the legal penalties, I should exercise it in this case.' Quite what he had in mind he did not reveal.

There was little Ralph could do. The prison chaplain told him that when Toby was bundled into a prison carriage and driven back to Ipswich Gaol after the trial, he saw through the bars the mail coach approaching.

'I beg you, let me be tied behind that coach that I may run for my life,' he cried.

'Who do you think you are, you black heathen?' the guard had growled. 'It's the hangman's noose for you.'

Toby was executed on 31 August. The villagers were pleased when the news came, but what they were really waiting for was the gibbeting.

On the morning of 14 September Ralph went to the crossroads on Blythburgh's heath. Stark against the sky, the newly erected gibbet awaited its gruesome burden. Ralph bowed his head in prayer. By noon a large crowd had gathered, eager for the spectacle. From Blythburgh, Walberswick, Southwold and all around they came. Anne's family stood slightly apart. Ralph hurried over to offer comfort.

As the tumbril rolled into view, a hush fell. Toby's tarred and iron-bound body was drawn up and suspended from the gibbet. When the corpse was revealed the crowd erupted into jeers and shouts. Mistress Blakemore was overcome, and Ralph sought to guide her away. Behind him came the neighing of panicked horses. Turning back, he saw one rear up, and a man fall. The man was named as a Mr Bokenham from Southwold. He didn't survive the day.

'Toby's claimed another life,' the rumour began. 'His evil spirit is walking.'

A year passed. Toby's grisly cadaver remained a source of both fascination and revulsion. Since Bokenham's death stories of unearthly apparitions had been shared around the fires in homes and hostelries.

'We were coming back along over the heath last even, John Price and me,' said Saul Blower to the company assembled in the White Hart. 'All of a sudden up behind us comes this carriage. Out of nowhere it came, bor. Threw ourselves down in the heather, we did, and that there carriage were pulled by horses with no hids, I swear to God.'

'I heard Matthew Todd had seen that too on the walks,' cried Jim Tuthill. 'Only, this one had a driver, a black man, and he had no hid neither!'

'You're daft, the lot of you,' called out the innkeeper. 'Why'd you go wandering up there at night, with that evil spirit clanking his chains and moaning?'

In the corner, Ralph stared morosely at his pie and despaired of his flock. They'd never stay at home, not with their nightly business on the coast to attend to.

The door opened, and Ralph smiled to see Mr Ward, the coroner. The village had not seen a crime that required a coroner since Toby, and Ralph had not seen Ward since before then.

'The people are working themselves into a frenzy with all this talk of phantoms,' Ralph said. 'Perhaps it is because they feel guilt for Toby's death. But justice had to be done, did it not?'

Coroner Ward put down his tankard. 'I hoped we'd not speak of that day. It still gives me nightmares.'

He spoke quietly. Ralph had to lean close to hear him. 'In all my years of holding inquests, I never felt afraid for my life till that day. They were so angry … My mind has been troubled ever since.'

'What do you mean?'

Ward lowered his voice further. 'If I was to say to you that there was not a mark on that young woman's body, what would you think?'

Ralph sat stunned. 'He swore to me that he was innocent.' He thought of Anne and those fits she'd suffered … 'Dear Lord, what have we done?'

After some wrangling with the authorities, Ralph arranged for Toby's remains to be taken down and buried near the gibbet. As he said a few words over the lonely grave he wished it could have been different. But Toby was a convicted murderer. There was no way he could be laid to rest in consecrated ground, was there?

Not long after, a tale reached Ralph's ears that some of Toby's fellow dragoons had removed the bones at dead of night and reburied them in the churchyard. He dismissed it as gossip – until he found a patch of roughly replaced turf below the east window.

'Toby, my lad, if you were wrongly served, then you are welcome here.'

When he heard rumours in the White Hart of a spectral carriage seen careering towards the churchyard wall then taking to the air and disappearing among the tombs, he smiled grimly to himself and offered up a prayer.

The stories of ghosts and the like might well have been just the talk of smugglers, to help clear the way for their night-time activities. A tale arose that poor Anne, safely buried in Walberswick churchyard, was walking too, as restless in death as in life. The sheep walks are long gone, the busy A12 thundering through them. Her shade flits between the cars and lorries on her endless unknown quest.

As for Toby, did he find peace or does his spirit roam the heathland still? A fragment of those old walks still bears his name. What was for a time a pretty and popular picnic site now lies desolate, tarred once more by association with activities undesirable to the locals. But the name stands as a memorial to a high-spirited young soldier, maybe guilty of no more than being in the wrong place at the wrong time.

3
The Treasure Seeker

When old Farmer Copping died, him who had the farm right next to Clopton Hall, near Wickhambrook, everyone reckoned that he must have treasure stashed away. Wasn't he a highly successful farmer, and a bachelor to boot? But when the new owner of the farm searched the house from top to bottom, he found nothing.

Three days after the old man's funeral, a farmworker walking by saw a tall, dark figure standing in the farmyard. If he hadn't been to the funeral and seen the coffin lowered into the ground, he'd have sworn it was Farmer Copping standing there, large as life. He yelled out and the figure vanished. It gave him quite a turn, but when he'd calmed down the farmworker realised what it meant. It was a sign! The treasure was buried in the farmyard. But when he and the other workers turned the yard over, no treasure did they find.

The new owner converted the farmhouse into workers' accommodation. The farmworker who'd seen the apparition moved in with his family, hoping that old Copping would show himself once more.

The farmworker had just the one child, Jack. He was a lazy lad who liked nothing more than to while away his time chucking stones into the pond by the lane. His mother despaired of him, but his father shook his head and said, 'If that old boy'd just show us where that treasure is, the lad could be as lazy as 'e loikes.'

One night Jack awoke to the sense that someone was watching him. When he opened his eyes, he saw a tall, dark figure looming over the bed. The figure reached out a hand to him and plucked at the bedclothes. Then it beckoned to him.

Jack was so scared that he just cried, 'Go away!' – and the figure vanished.

Jack had some trouble getting to sleep the next night. In his mind's eye he saw, over and over, the dark figure reaching down. At last he did sleep, but moments later, it seemed, his eyes opened and there, once more, was the tall, dark figure. It was reaching down and it tugged the blanket half off him and beckoned.

'Go away!' cried Jack.

Once more the figure vanished.

The third night Jack lay awake, hoping that if he did the apparition wouldn't come. To no avail. It bent right over him, beckoning, and the bedclothes were all over the floor …

'Go away, damn you!' cried Jack.

The figure vanished and at that same moment Jack's father burst through the door.

'What're you yelling about?'

Still full of terror, Jack explained what had happened the last three nights. If he'd been expecting sympathy he was disappointed.

'You mazy fool,' cried his dad. 'That'll have been the old boy, wanting to show you – *you*, Jack – the treasure, and now you've blown it!'

Blown it Jack had, for the tall, dark figure never troubled him again. Jack was furious with himself. He threw a good many more stones into the pond over the next few years. Without the treasure, he became a farmworker like his dad. There was hardly a day went by when he didn't chastise himself for throwing up the opportunity of living like a gentleman who didn't have to work.

Then one night he was in the White Horse in Wickhambrook and a friend was telling a tale he'd heard off a Melford man.

''E said there was a grut battle between Melford and Acton, with that Boadicea trouncing them Romans, the Ninth Legion, 'e said, and their treasure was all stolen, save for one chest o' gold, and thas wholly lost, as there's a ghostie guarding that in Wimbrell Pond!'

Jack laughed along with everyone else, but as he was walking home it struck him. Treasure guarded by a ghost! Ghosts were sitting on treasure

– treasure that he could win! Hadn't he already seen one ghost? He'd not be frit again! The next day he went back to his friend and got the whole story out of him. He came home all fired up with excitement. He began to read up on the subject, reckoning that if there were two ghosts hiding treasure within a few miles of each other, then there must be more.

His hunch was right. There was so much hidden treasure out there that he was quids in – if he could just get past the ghosts! So he quit his job, packed a bag, and with a shovel on his back, and a Bible in his pocket, off he set.

His first port of call was that Roman ghost down at Acton. His friend had been quite specific, and Jack soon found his way to Nursery Corner on the Acton road. On one side was the new railway from Sudbury, running across marshy ground thick with alders. Behind him was a gravel pit, across the road he could see the walls of Acton Place, and there, in the field next to the hall, was a large round pool, the moonlight glinting on it. Wimbrell Pond.

He checked his tools – a long stick and a stone – then over the road he crept. He jumped the ditch and scrambled up the bank. When he got to the pond he lobbed the stone in. Immediately he heard the dink of stone hitting metal. Without hesitating, he was in the pond, wading through the water, poking the stick to find the treasure chest.

Right in the centre of the pond his stick hit something hard. It had to be the chest! He reached down into the water and hauled it up. No sooner had he done so than a burst of cold rushed through him, far colder than the water. It left him juddering. When he looked up, he saw wavering in front of him a figure. It quavered in the breeze among shreds of mist, barely discernible as human in form. It had dark hollows where its eyes should be, and these it fixed on the chest in Jack's hands.

'That's mine!' it cried.

Jack dropped the chest and vaulted out of the water, over the ditch and across the road. He could see the figure floating above the pond, and that sent him legging it back up the road to Melford.

By the time he was walking back up to the town he'd calmed down and was berating himself for his cowardice. Still, he knew exactly where the treasure was. All he had to do was go back and get it … in the daylight. Back he went at dawn. Checking for any sign of the more earthly dangers of gamekeepers or farmers, he returned to the pond, waded into the middle, reached down … but found nothing! He searched the whole pond, but there was no sign. He realised that there was a strange logic to this: you could only get the treasure from the ghost himself.

The next night he was back, stick and stone and all, but when he threw in the stone there was no sound save for splashing water, his stick found no chest and the ghost failed to appear. Three nights he tried it. He realised that once more he'd blown it.

Disheartened, he checked his maps. What he spotted raised his spirits. It was surely a sign! Slap bang in the middle of the county was another Clopton! A home from home, with its own hidden treasure.

This Clopton was near Rattlesden, so he made his way to the Half Moon pub and asked over a beer about the treasure.

An old boy in the corner piped up: 'Thas from St Felix, that is. They say that when St Felix brought religion to Suffolk he brought treasure as well, and some o' that he hid up by Clopton Hall, leaving a monk and a dog to guard it.'

Jack set off that night with his shovel on his back and a bellyful of confidence from the beer. Past Cloptongreen Farm he crept, then into the woods by the Hall where the old boys had said the ghost lurked. Strange, he thought, that they'd said 'ghost', when surely there were two? A dog and a monk. In the woods he heard something. Was it … a yip? The dog? He steeled himself, shovel in hand. From out of the undergrowth leapt a glowing figure. His blood ran cold. This was no dog, but a monk in habit and sandals and all, but with the head of a dog, barking and yapping at him. Yowling as loud as the dog, away Jack ran.

After he'd collected himself, he berated himself once more. He'd blown it again. When he went back the next night the woods were empty of ghosts but full of gamekeepers, so that was that.

But he was determined not to give up. Next stop was yet another Clopton. Oddly, this one, near Grundisburgh, had the same story of St Felix, the monk and the dog. That just made it easier. He'd seen it all before.

But as he crept up Whitefoot Lane it was no dog-headed monk that emerged from the shadows and chased him down the hill back to Burgh, it was a lolloping monk-headed dog!

At nearby Dallinghoo he searched for the much safer option of an ordinary human ghost guarding a treasure by a high gatepost, but he couldn't find the gatepost, let alone the ghost.

By now he was on the verge of giving up. He'd not made a penny! He checked his notes one last time. Something he saw there made him smile, hoist his pack on his back and start walking south and east to Orford. He went straight to the Jolly Sailor near the quay and asked about the treasure.

'There's a witch I've read about,' he said. 'A witch with lots of gold.'

The locals looked at each other, then an old boy spoke up: 'They do say she was overly fond of gold, that one, and wouldn't be paid in anything less! And when that'un died they buried her gold with her. But she didn't rest easy, with the weight of all that gold on her, so she started walking betwixt church and castle, and giving that gold away …'

Jack didn't stop to hear more. He left so fast he didn't hear the sniggering from the bar.

In the dead of night he made his way from his lodgings up to the castle. It stood tall and dark on its hill, almost smothered by the darkness. At the other end of Market Hill he could just see the church. He walked towards it, hoping against hope …

Suddenly, right in front of him appeared a glowing, dark figure. An old woman with a furious expression on her face, holding in her right hand a pointed stick and in her left a bag.

She glided up to him, and cried, 'Take this here stick and bury this here gold. Don't that'll be the worse for you!'

He took the stick, he took the bag and, as he did, she vanished. Quick as you like he was off back up to Castle Green, in through the gate and digging with the stick. Soon the gold was safely in the ground. He left the stick poking out as a marker.

When he came back the next day there wasn't the smallest sign of stick, gold or even disturbed earth. Shaking his head, he thought he must've misplaced the spot, and resolved to try again.

Sure enough, when he walked up Market Hill there was the old woman.

'Take this here stick and bury this here gold …'

He buried the gold and marked the spot with a primrose flower. Once again in the morning there was no sign.

A third night he went out, and there she was. He took stick and gold and off he went, but no sooner had he buried the gold than she was there again, thrusting more into his hands. He buried that too. On his way home he met her a third time, but as he was burying that gold he spotted another figure. In the moonlight it looked like this person had a pointed stick as well!

He hurried over to them, and found, pointed stick in one hand and bag in the other, a young woman looking confused.

'I was out on an errand,' she said, 'and this old woman thrust these into my hands …'

The next morning at dawn the two of them arranged to meet up, but neither of them could find any of the gold.

'There's something not right here,' said the woman, Mary, who was a maid in a house on Market Hill. 'I think we've been conned.'

It was plain that Mary wasn't the kind of girl who took being conned lightly. That evening the two of them went to the Jolly Sailor and told their tale. The old boys looked at each other and shook their heads.

'Thas gettin' too much now,' said the old boy who'd told the tale. 'That ol' ghost's gone doolally.'

The rector was called for to lay the ghost.

Jack and Mary were there as the rector tussled the spirit up to the churchyard. Jack watched him forcing that spirit underneath an iron bar in the ruins behind the church, and vowed that he'd not mix with the supernatural again.

Back to his Clopton Green home and his job as a farmworker he went, but in the end he didn't go back empty-handed. It wasn't gold he took with him but something that he always said was far better – he took Mary to be his wife. She'd told him how she'd once defeated a ghost in the house where she worked, and he reckoned to himself that a woman like that was just what he needed, in case that old Farmer Copping came back to trouble him.

4

These Lovers Fled Away

Dot and Josie were typical eight-year-old chatterboxes. On that Sunday afternoon in October 1935 they were in high spirits. They'd been on a walk with Dot's mother and were looking forward to tea at her grandmother's in Mustow Street, especially her famous cakes. They'd walked out along the Barton Road beyond the edge of Bury St Edmunds. Now they were coming back down Eastgate Street. There were still gaps between the houses giving views of the fields.

Ahead was the old railway bridge. No trains had run there since the Great War, and it was dark and gloomy underneath.

'Come along, you two,' chivvied Dot's mum as they neared the arch.

Just then something caught Josie's eye in the field across the road.

'What are those funny-looking people doing?' she asked.

Dot and her mother looked where she pointed.

In the field were a man and woman dressed in strangely summery clothes, the woman in a long dress and the man in a loose, light-coloured shirt and trousers.

'They look like they're in fancy dress,' giggled Dot.

Josie dug her in the ribs. 'There's something wrong about them.'

The two people were coming towards them, but moving slowly and erratically. The man was leaning heavily on the woman, who was struggling under his weight.

'Shouldn't we go and help?' asked Josie.

At that, Dot's mum gasped, and grabbed their coat sleeves to stop them dashing across the road.

They watched the couple reach the road and make their painful way across. Dot and Josie shivered as a strong, cold wind seemed to come out of nowhere. They could see now that that the woman was wearing an old-fashioned nurse's uniform. The man looked like he was in his nightshirt!

As the couple stepped on to the road, a car suddenly appeared. Josie cried out, and felt Dot's mum's grip on her arm tighten. The car ground to a halt, and the driver jumped out, swearing and brandishing his starting handle. But, neither the couple nor he paid any attention to each other. They kept crossing and he started cranking his engine, which didn't respond.

The strange couple were only a few yards from Dot and Josie now. The girls shivered in the increasing cold. Dot's mum's grip remained very tight as the couple began to scramble up the bank. They were clearly exhausted. The man was dragging his leg. The woman was talking, but the wind seemed to blow the words away. The girls felt rooted to the spot, as if something besides Dot's mum was stopping them moving.

The man and woman reached the top of the slope where the field bordered some shrubby woodland known as 'The Glen'. Upon reaching the trees they disappeared from view. The girls immediately felt released, and Dot's mum pulled them sternly on.

'Hurry up – we'll be late for tea.'

They heard the car sputter into life and drive off. Dot and Josie hardly noticed passing under the dark railway arch. As they emerged through to the other side, the wind dropped.

In the summer of 1854 Mary Treese left her home village near Bury and went into town to help nurse the wounded soldiers coming home from the Crimea. Her father was none too pleased.

'There's plenty of work needs doing on the farm,' he said. 'Girls should stay home, not gad off on their own, and a young unmarried lass like you nursing young men is downright indecent.'

But off she went anyway. The hospital, in a large house on the north side of town, was soon full. Mary had to learn fast. She was no stranger to blood and injuries, thanks to life on the farm, but what she faced now was hard to take. The amputations, the wounds that would not heal, the despair. She became strong, always kept a smile on her face. Sometimes that smile was the only medicine she could give.

There was one man for whom her smile became brighter. At first, she'd felt sorry for him. His leg had been fractured by a musket ball at Inkerman, and the patching up in a Turkish military hospital hadn't helped much. Bury wasn't his home, nor even England, as his Irish brogue made plain. He'd been recruited by the 63rd West Suffolks when they'd been stationed in Cork.

Mary knew she shouldn't have favourites. Matron was very strict on that. But Connor had no family to visit him, and she loved to hear him speak about his home, and the family farm that sounded so like hers.

'Ireland sounds beautiful,' she said when he described the lush green fields and hills.

'Aye, and when I'm well, me darlin', I'll take ye there, so I will, and ye can see for yourself.' He clasped her hand for a moment as he said it. Mary's heart skipped, and she squeezed back.

Back at the farm on her days off, she was determined to speak of her work in the hospital.

'The patients are so grateful. It's a gift when they recover.'

Before she knew it, she was telling them about Connor. She felt her cheeks heat as she did, and saw her mother look fearfully at her husband.

Farmer Treese banged his fist on the table. 'Connor? What sort of a name is that? It's foreign, that's what that is, and he's spinning you a likely yarn, my girl. Thinks he can lure you away with his fancy talk, does he? Not while I have breath he won't. If he lays a finger on you I'll be after him with my gun.'

A few days later, back at the hospital, she had a visit from her brother, Rob.

'Da's in a rare old temper,' he warned. 'If you don't come home he'll be over here to get you.'

Mary was furious with him, and her da, and then, to top it all, she was summoned to Matron's office.

'Nurse Treese, your father has requested your return home. The tale he tells is very disappointing. You know you must not consort with the men.'

Mary stared at her, the fury mounting.

To her surprise, Matron's face softened. 'You're a good worker, and I do not wish to lose you. If I allow you to remain against your father's wish, your behaviour must be exemplary. You will not be treating Private Flynn again – he'll be transferred tomorrow.'

Outside the office, Mary's heart was racing. Those few short words from Matron had made everything clear. She could not leave Connor. She loved him.

She crept to his ward after dark, put her finger to her lips when he would have greeted her.

He immediately sensed something was wrong. 'What is it, Mary, mavourneen?'

'How far do you think you can walk now?' she whispered. His face fell, but she ploughed on. 'They're going to send you away, or me … We have to get away from here. I've got a plan. A bit of one, anyway. First thing tomorrow, I'm coming to get you … if you can walk.'

'Mary, I'll try. I don't know how far …' He suddenly gripped her hand in his, and she saw in his eyes an echo of her own feelings. 'I'll not lose you.'

Before it was light, Mary came into the ward. A whispered word to the night nurse about an errand sent the girl scurrying away. Connor was awake. She eased him out of bed. He could put his weight on the leg now, and they made good progress through the building. Mary had left her bag and a blanket ready on a hook by the back door. She threw the blanket over his shoulders. Then they were out, and slipping away down the lane to the fields beyond.

The leg that had seemed almost mended in the hospital didn't hold up well on the rough, damp October grass, but Connor didn't complain. They had to make a big loop to find a way across the river.

They huddled under a tree to eat the bread and cheese from Mary's bag. Mary could see the hollowness of his eyes, but refused to admit to herself that she'd made a mistake. As they walked on a chill wind got up, gaining in strength, even as Connor's strength was fading.

'How much further, Mary?'

She took his face in her hands and lifted his tired head. His eyes were … not defeated … resigned. She took a deep breath, and put on her hospital smile.

'Look, there's some woods ahead, see, on that bit of a hill. If we can reach there we can rest till morning. There's a road above the wood that goes out of town and I've money for the stagecoach. Think of your Irish hills, Connor. We'll see them yet, you and me.'

Her words seemed to give him new strength. There was a field, then a road to cross, the wind tugging at them. The blanket blew away, but Mary couldn't rescue it. Connor was leaning heavily on her now.

'Nearly there,' she gasped.

In the cover of the trees Mary eased Connor down against a tree trunk and attended to his leg bandage. She couldn't look into his face, so grey with exhaustion was it. She'd been a fool to think he was fit –

The snap of twigs made them both look up.

Standing right in front of them was Mary's father, gun in hand and face contorted with fury.

'Thought you could steal my daughter, did you, you dirty bog-trotter?'

Mary flung herself at her father's feet. 'No, Father, no!' she screeched. 'You don't understand. We love each other –'

Her words were killed by the gunshot. She wheeled around and screamed. Connor lay limp against the tree, blood spilling from his chest, his eyes empty.

Moments later there was a sergeant on the scene and Farmer Treese was taken away. Mary pieced together the story afterwards. The alarm raised at the hospital when they realised they'd gone. A sergeant of the regiment was summoned and a search party sent out. Then her father had arrived, demanding to take her home. When he learnt of their disappearance he seized the shotgun from under the seat of his trap and set out by himself to find her. He found an old man who'd seen them, and drove on towards Eastgate. Then he'd spotted them climbing the bank to the wood.

In those days there was only one penalty for murder.

Mary never returned home. Her family shunned her, blaming her for her father's hanging. Indeed, she blamed herself, could hardly bear to be in her own skin. When the call came from Florence Nightingale for nurses to go out to the Crimea she took ship straight away. Nursing became her life. When the war was done, she stayed nursing, but wouldn't go back to Suffolk. She took herself to the Irish hills Connor had told her about, and that is where she stayed.

Still shivering, Dot and Josie hurried along Eastgate Street after Dot's mum.

'Those people were odd,' Dot ventured at last. 'Like they didn't even see us. Like they weren't quite there.'

Her mother pursed her lips and said nothing.

'I'm going to tell Grandma about it,' said Dot. 'She knows everything.'

Then, behind them, from the direction of The Glen, came a loud, sharp bang. The girls stopped dead and looked at each other. It had sounded for all the world like a gun.

'Just someone after rabbits?' said Josie, but she grabbed hold of Dot's hand.

Then came the scream, a woman's anguished scream that went on and on. Dot's mother stood and stared, but the girls turned and ran and they didn't stop till they reached Grandma's house.

5

The Rougham Mirage

That August bank holiday weekend in 1980 began early for Tamsy Johnson and her mum Penny. They'd been among the first to arrive at the Rougham estates. With practised hands they'd got their tepee up, their sheepskins spread out, their beds made and a fire lit. During term time they lived in a little terraced house in Ipswich, but throughout the summer holidays Tamsy and her mum travelled the camps and fairs up and down the country. This weekend was the Rougham Tree Fair, one of the East Anglian Albion fairs. They'd already been to the Moon Fair at East Bergholt and the Sun Fair at Lyng and were looking forward to catching up with friends.

At eleven, Tamsy was well used to this kind of life. She'd been toted around fairs and camps since she was a baby. Some of the kids at school mocked her for being a hippy, but really, who wouldn't like running free in a pack of friends all day and well into the night? Who wouldn't like seeing jugglers and mime and taking part in dancing and acrobatics, in crafts and art? And there was always an adult nearby to mop up tears and apply plasters to grazed knees.

That first day, however, Tamsy was bored. None of her friends had arrived yet and everybody was too busy setting up camp to do anything fun. The smell of resin permeated the camp from all the sawing, but Tamsy's heart sank when she got back to her tepee and smelt another distinctive scent coming from inside. When she pushed the flap open, she saw her mum sitting smoking with a couple of long-haired blokes Tamsy didn't know, one of them strumming a lute. Her mum looked up, guilt all over her face. Tamsy dropped the flap down in disgust.

Moments later, her mum was outside, but she was off on one, Tamsy could see, swaying to the lute music filtering out from the tepee.

'Mum, do you *have* to?' moaned Tamsy. 'It makes you stupid.'

Penny turned her face to the sun. 'It's so beautiful.'

Tamsy scowled, and her mum went on hurriedly, 'Let's go out. Let's go and explore.'

Grinning, Tamsy ducked back into the tent. In the face of the men's baffled stares, she threw into her bag a thermos of water, some of her mum's flapjacks and the blue 1:25,000 OS map she'd got her mum to buy for the weekend. Then she and her mum shugged on their Glastonbury boots, Tamsy's with a pattern of the Tor, her mum's with mushrooms.

They followed a lime walk down to the church. To Tamsy's embarrassment, her mum started to dance around the tombs.

'Come *on*,' she cried, beckoning her to the footpath she'd chosen.

'You shouldn't follow the maps,' her mum said dreamily. 'You should follow where your heart wants you to go …'

They marched across a field, then sat against a hedge in the heat to eat a flapjack, Tamsy plotting the course for a circular walk back to the camp. Then they were off again, past the Royal Oak pub, over a road and down a leafy lane. Penny picked some scabious and ox-eye daisies and wove them into coronets for them both.

Tamsy was expecting the lane to open into a field, but to her surprise a high wall of Cambridgeshire yellow brick rose up, damp and green with algae. She stared at the map.

'This shouldn't be here!'

'Just go with the flow,' murmured her mum.

As they walked along the wall the air grew chillier in the shade. They came to some fancy iron gates, all shiny and new-looking. The gates were slightly ajar, so they peered inside. Beyond a carefully landscaped lawn, through tall trees, they glimpsed a four-square red brick house.

'That's Georgian,' said Penny.

Tamsy didn't know what that meant. An architectural discussion carried them past the yellow brick wall back into the sunshine. They could see what the map said was Bradfield St George's church ahead of them.

'Better get back,' said Penny, gesturing at the sinking sun. 'We need to sort through my face paints for tomorrow, and I promised I'd cook for Bob and Peter tonight.'

She produced a packet containing a couple of brown homemade biscuits. Tamsy thought they tasted strange, but ate hers up.

They turned a corner and began to walk back up the road. Tamsy looked out for the house they'd seen, since their way back took them parallel to the way they'd come, but there was nothing across the field except a dark copse of pine trees. She checked the map. That was actually correct. Weird.

As they walked along in the warmth of the late afternoon sun, there was a sudden whooshing noise. Tamsy's ears popped. Suddenly it was really cold. They shivered in their sleeveless tops and stared around them in bewilderment. The light was weird, too: a thick mist was settling around them, but the sun was shining brightly through it.

'Mum …' murmured Tamsy.

Penny put her arm around Tamsy's shoulders, saying, 'It's all right, flower.' But her voice sounded uncertain.

Tamsy looked around and gasped.

There, lit by the bright misty light, was the house they'd seen. She was sure it hadn't been there a moment ago; just the copse of trees. A Georgian house, red brick, three storeys high with huge rectangular windows. Its gardens spilled out in serried ranks of bright flowers and dark shrubs.

While they stood staring, the mist deepened and swallowed the house. Then, just as suddenly as it had come, the mist – and the house – vanished, leaving them standing by the road in the sunshine staring at that copse of trees.

'What was in those biscuits, Mum?' whispered Tamsy.

'Just carob!'

They walked briskly back to the camp and busied themselves sorting out the face-painting kit and chopping vegetables. Bob and Pete showed up with bottles of red wine, full of talk about erecting the Albion stage, and how this person and that had arrived. Tamsy and Penny let them talk. They didn't say anything about what they'd seen.

In the morning Tamsy's friends arrived. After Penny had painted all their faces with butterflies and rainbows, they raced off to bounce on

the bouncy castle, to dance among the rainbow, tie-dyed people, and to buy paper yo-yos and shoot them out at unsuspecting passers-by. That night Tamsy stayed up late with her friends watching the bands, dancing and talking, but when she fell asleep she saw the house once more in her dreams.

The next morning she woke up early and decided that she had to know. Very quietly, she slipped out of bed, tugged on clothes and boots, stuffed a roll and an apple in her pack and went out to retrace her steps of two days before.

She made her way down the lane to where they'd seen the brick wall, then stopped dead. There was no yellow wall! Just a stubbly field smelling slightly of ash with a path down to the copse they'd seen from the road.

'I knew it wasn't on the map,' Tamsy cried, and set off along the path.

The copse looked forbidding, a dark mass of pines. She took a deep breath and slipped inside the trees. There was a bank all the way around, on which a few oaks and hawthorns were growing, then a ditch, and then the ranks of pine trees. She scrambled over the bank and began to root about, not really knowing what she was looking for. Then, sticking from the earth, she saw a chunk of brick. Yellow brick, crumbling with age.

She picked it up and stared at it.

'So it *was* here,' she said. 'But when?'

She stuffed the piece of brick in her pocket. No sooner had she done so than there was a huge bang and the wood billowed with smoke. Tamsy screamed, terrified that there was a man with a gun. She *was* trespassing!

She shot out of the copse as if the Devil was after her and ran all the way back to the road, where she ran smack-bang into an old man.

'Watch where you're going!' he cried, as she flailed away from him.

As she caught her breath she saw him taking in her cheesecloth shirt and brightly coloured boots. 'Where've you been to be running in such a hurry?'

Tamsy burst out, 'I went to find the house! We saw it – but it's not there!'

To her surprise, the old man's face turned from suspicion to understanding.

'On Kingshall Street?' he asked. 'Red brick house, gardens, all that?'

Tamsy nodded and explained what she'd seen, and the old man nodded away until she mentioned the shotgun noise.

'Them bird-scarers! You shouldn't have gone in there, but children will be children. You're not the first to see that house, you know. People've been seeing it more than a century now. Saw it myself back in the war when I was a young'un, just like you said, with all that mist, but it were winter when I saw it, and the flowers were still blooming …'

Tamsy thoughtfully made her way back to the fair. It was still early, everyone still getting up. After breakfast, she found her friends again. If she was a little quiet that day, they didn't comment on it.

When they packed up on Monday afternoon, Tamsy carefully stowed her piece of yellow brick. At home she put it up on a shelf with her other treasures. She didn't exactly forget what they'd seen, but her mother never mentioned it and as time moved on Tamsy began to think she'd imagined it. The following year she was twelve and not so interested in maps or walking; boys and dancing took up her time at the fair instead. The following year, 1982, was the last Tree Fair held at Rougham. Tamsy had no cause to go there after that. The piece of brick was chucked away in a house move when she was fifteen.

She studied architecture at university and then moved back to East Anglia to work in Bury. It wasn't until 2007 that she had cause to think of the house again. Waiting one day to pick up her daughter from school, she was idly flicking through the *East Anglian Daily Times* when an article made her freeze. She read that a woman, a Mrs Bartram, had driven to Rougham from Bradfield St George and, on the very same road, Kingshall Street, had seen that house. The article described it exactly: a Georgian red brick house with formal gardens out the front. Trembling, Tamsy read about the other reports, from Robert Palfreys seeing the house in 1860 to Ruth Wynne seeing the yellow wall in the 1920s. Her mind was transported back to that summer, and the sight of that house rising out of the mist lit by that strange, unearthly light.

6

The Lowestoft Witches

In the 1880s, business was booming in Lowestoft's beach village. There were plenty of herring in the sea, the gas works was flourishing and the beach companies were thriving. To cope with all the traffic, Whapload Road, which ran along the top of the village, needed widening. A group of workmen were hired and began the backbreaking work of digging. They worked their way along the road, supping at a different tavern each night, until they came to the bottom of Wilde's Score.

The men were joking and laughing as they dug. Suddenly, the foreman, Dick Ayers, cried, 'Stop!'

The men all froze mid-shovel.

'We've found a body, boys!'

The men peered down, and there, sure enough, was the smooth round shape of a skull.

'Dig careful now,' said Dick. 'He'll have to come up.'

Most of the men were no strangers to finding grisly stuff in the ground. One of the crew joked about how he'd been working inland last year and they'd hit a cow skull. They'd backed out of there pretty fast, he said. Everyone nodded. Everyone save young Ed Prettyman, whose first labouring job this was.

His eyes were fixed on the emerging skeleton. God, couldn't they just leave it in the ground? Surely he'd be happy with the new road over him? He must have spoken that out loud, because the men started laughing.

'That's no man, Ed,' laughed Dick. 'Not with hips like that. You'd better be learning the difference, or you're going to get in lots of trouble!'

Ed, blushing, turned his attention back to the skeleton. Her mouth had fallen wide open, as if she too was laughing at him. Then something caught his eye.

'What's that?' he asked.

'Them's bones, boy,' laughed Dick, but as he looked where Ed was pointing his laughter cut off.

Right through her knees, ankles and elbows were huge, rusty pins.

Dick swore and hopped out of the grave fast.

'Get a clergyman here, quick. That's no ordinary grave. That's a witch!'

Everyone dropped their shovels and leapt out, backing away as fast as they could. Ed backed the furthest, racing away to Christchurch.

'Mr Lancaster, Mr Lancaster, we've found a witch!'

Mr Lancaster was a very calm man. With Ed bobbing behind him like a chick, he marched to the grave, which had by now attracted a small crowd of onlookers.

'You don't believe that superstitious nonsense do you, lads? Whoever this unfortunate was, and whatever she did, she deserves a good Christian burial now. Dig her up and bring her to the church, and I'll see it done. Now, all you lot – clear away and let these men work!'

Job done, the men made their way to the closest pub, the Gas House Tavern.

After a couple of pints to quench their thirst, one of the men, Sam Lark, said, 'I reckon I know who that was. I reckon it was Amy Denny!'

The men all nodded nervously and supped their beer faster. All except Ed.

'Who's Amy Denny?'

The men, as one, stopped drinking.

'How is it,' mused Sam, 'that a man, Lowestoft born and bred, doesn't know about Amy Denny and Rose Cullender? You must know about the witches' stones by the park?'

Ed nodded. Everyone knew the stones, they were at the top of Belle Vue Park on everyone's way out of town, and he did remember someone saying that a witch used to sit there and that's why the stones were cursed to roll down to the sea every midnight. But he didn't know the names.

'Tell us the story, then,' he said.

Sam shook his head. "'Tis not a story for after dark.'

But at the end of the next day Sam came to Ed with a grubby little book.

'You read this,' he said, 'and you'll understand.'

The pamphlet told the tale of a witch trial more than 200 years before.

The whole sorry affair started when Amy Denny suckled a child. She was an old woman, long past childbearing, but old women looking after children often offered a breast to comfort a child. People said it gave the babes wind, but that wasn't why Dorothy Durrant objected to the suckling of her child. People were already whispering that Amy Denny was a witch. Back in the 1650s the word 'witch' was very much on people's lips. The trials conducted by the self-styled Witchfinder General, Matthew Hopkins, had only been twenty years before and, though some didn't believe in witches, far more did. Amy was a prime suspect. Since she and her husband had come over from Beccles they'd been nothing but trouble. John Denny had been up before the magistrate sixty-nine times before his death, and Amy wasn't much more law-abiding.

The child she'd suckled took sick. His mother sent all the way to Yarmouth for a doctor known to cure bewitchments. He took one look at the child and told Dorothy to hang the child's blanket by the fire. 'After a day, wrap the child in it and if anything falls out throw it straight in the fire!'

What fell out was a huge toad. They threw it into the flames, where it burnt right up. A rumour ran around that Amy's neighbours had found her that day with burns on her face and legs even though she had no fire in the house!

Furious at the accusations, Amy accosted Dorothy.

Afterwards, Dorothy told her neighbours that Amy had cursed her. 'She said one of my children would die, and that I'd go lame!'

Within the year Amy's curse had come true.

Dorothy wasn't the only one to make accusations. On the High Street, right next to Wilde's Score, lived Samuel Pacy, prosperous fish merchant and an influential man in the town. Amy Denny came to his house to buy herring, but was turned away. She was soon back, and was turned away once more, and then a third time. Pacy could hear her muttering as she stamped down Wilde's Score.

That day his daughter Deborah, who hadn't been feeling well, had asked to be carried out to their long garden to look out at the sea. As soon as Amy had gone the third time, Deborah screamed. They found her lying on her side, gripping her stomach.

'It feels like the pricking of pins,' she whispered.

Pacy's elder daughter Elizabeth, not to be outdone, started to complain of the same pains. Both children had fits. They would spit up pins, the very pins that pained them. They would cry out that Amy Denny and another woman, Rose Cullender, stood at their bedhead conjuring the pins into their bodies.

Deborah and Elizabeth were the first, but soon other girls in the town were afflicted. All blamed Amy and this Rose Cullender.

When Rose and her daughter Susan heard the news, they were shocked. Rose was a widow, but she wasn't poor. She certainly didn't know the likes of Amy Denny. The only time she'd had anything to do with the Pacys was to try to buy fish from them!

But Rose was another known to be trouble. Where she lived, Swan Lane, the road was very narrow, and as often as not carts would scrape against her house. It'd happened so often that whenever Rose heard the carts rumbling by, she would rush out into the street and rant at the carters.

The carters started to tell tales.

One said that after his cart had touched her house the cart got stuck in a gate.

When others laughed he went on, 'No, seriously, we couldn't get it through and had to cut down the gate posts, even though the cart wasn't touching them. And those who came to help us unload all got nose bleeds. That's cursing, that is.'

Another said that, yes, maybe he'd clipped the side of her house, but she'd come out and started cursing. 'She swore the horses would suffer, and d'you know – three of 'em were dead within the week!'

Witch fever gripped the town.

Women came to Rose's house. They stripped her and searched her body for witchmarks. They found an extra nipple on her belly, and other marks beside. It proved that she was a witch for sure.

Rose was arrested and bundled into a wagon with Amy. Irons were set on their wrists. Rose's daughter Susan tried to stop the men, screaming that her mother had done no wrong. It was no good. The men shoved her away, and she backed off, weeping.

A crowd gathered, their faces ugly with hate. The two women stared dumbly as these people they'd known for years jeered them out of town.

'Child-killers!'

'Witches!'

'May you burn in hell!'

When they were clear of the town, Amy leaned over and hissed at Rose, 'Did you do it?'

Numbly Rose shook her head.

'You?'

For a moment Amy looked as if she was going to make some bravura comment, but then her shoulders slumped and she shook her head.

Prison was bad. It was cold. Filthy. The other women shunned them as child-killers and unholy witches.

The trial was far worse. The judge looked at them with disgust in his eyes. The awful litany of things they were said to have done went on and on. Children were brought in and screamed in their presence. Neither woman had anyone to speak for them. They knew they had no hope.

They were found guilty, and were hanged on Thingoe Hill in Bury on 17 March 1662.

Their bodies were brought back to Lowestoft. No one knew now where they were buried, but witches were never buried in consecrated ground. They were buried near the scene of their crimes, weren't they? And wasn't Wilde's Score right next to the Pacys' house?

Ed stared at the book and shivered.

He thought of his own granny who lived all alone save for her cat down in the beach village. She had a crotchety tongue … but no one was afraid of her, were they? No one would call her a witch, would they?

The people who'd pinned down that skeleton had been afraid. Ed wasn't a fool. He knew they'd been afraid the witch would walk.

The next evening, after a long hard day working on the new road in the rain, Ed turned up Wilde's Score to make his way home to Mariner's Street. It was still wet, so he hurried along. As he neared the top, he heard something.

An old woman's voice called out, 'Help me!'

She sounded close by.

He swung round in the darkness, but couldn't see anything. 'Who's there?'

'Help me …'

Worried now, Ed knocked on the nearest door. Light and warmth flooded out, and a woman stared at him.

'I heard an old woman,' he said. 'She sounded as if she was in trouble.'

Soon the score was full of men with lanterns calling out and searching, but they found nothing.

The woman Ed had spoken to lingered as the men ducked back into their homes.

'You're one of them workmen that dug up the skeleton, aren't you?' she said. 'I reckon I know who it was you heard. You lot raised Amy Denny – and now she's walking!'

With that she slammed the door in his face.

For a moment Ed stood there in the rain and the darkness, his skin crawling, then he ducked down his head and hurried on to the High Street. He set a swift pace to Mariner's Street and turned down it in relief.

To his surprise, a woman was out in the rain ahead of him. She was dressed in a long, hooded cloak. Sensible wet weather gear. But Ed froze. The woman was glowing. For a long moment they stood there, the glowing figure and the young man, and then she was gone, leaving the street in darkness.

When Ed got inside, he stammered out everything to his mum.

She laughed. 'Oh lad, you do know what Mariner's Street used to be called, don't you? It was Swan Lane.' She smiled at his shocked face. 'That's right – where Rose Cullender used to live. Maybe she's risen in sympathy with her sister …'

The next day Ed gave the pamphlet back to Sam and in a whisper told him what he'd seen and heard.

Sam cast a worried look up to Wilde's Score, but he said, 'You've got some imagination, haven't you?'

Ed could see Sam wasn't convinced. But he was sure of what he'd seen. That lunchtime he jacked in his job on the road and walked up to the river. Then and there he signed on to a trading wherry heading down the coast. He didn't come back to Lowestoft for a very long time.

7

The Constant Maid

It was 21 May 1672. Bessie was on the Southwold cliffs to see the English and French fleets sail back into Sole Bay. It was almost festive, despite the fears of a new war with the Dutch. There had been weeks of harassment by the Dutch. A privateer had attacked a Southwold ketch off the Norfolk coast, and ships had been spotted patrolling the bay.

The whole town seemed to be there to cheer the Duke of York's flagship *Prince* in, but Bessie's heart started racing when she saw, at last, the ship she had waited seven years for, the *Royal James* commanded by Edward Montagu, Earl of Sandwich.

Bessie had been just fourteen when she went into service in 1665 at Cammells on the High Street, one of the few houses to survive the Southwold fire in 1659. She was nervous of such a fine place at first, but when she was busy upstairs she'd look out of the windows and pretend she was the lady of the house, awaiting her dashing husband.

Almost as soon as she started, the house had noble visitors, for the duke and the earl used it as their headquarters while the fleet was in Sole Bay during the last Dutch war. She'd been dazzled by these noblemen with their grand clothes and their way of speaking, so foreign to her Suffolk ears. But she held up her chin and always made sure her fine red hair was a little bit visible under her cap.

The duke barely knew she was there, but Lord Montagu always took the time to ask how she was. Although she'd never learnt to read, she was fascinated by all the charts spread out on his table. Sometimes he would point to things and try to explain. His words went over her head, but she was glad to gaze at his noble features as he bent earnestly over the charts. He was a well-built man, clean shaven apart from a small moustache, with a strong straight nose and dark brown eyes. And he was not all seriousness. There were many dances, when the house came alive with music. At the first dance, she was astonished to see the earl playing the guitar. He looked up, and to Bessie it was as if his eyes were on her alone. She smiled back, her heart aflutter. So delicious a feeling.

That June there was a sea battle off Lowestoft, and Lord Montagu returned victorious. Bessie could see the exhilaration in his eyes. He caught her up and twirled her around. As she gazed into his dark eyes and felt his strong hands on her waist she almost swooned.

'Oh, my lord,' she breathed.

He set her down with a playful pat on her behind.

'Ale, Bessie, our throats are parched,' he said, and she was just a servant once more.

When he returned to Southwold in September, he was a different man. A scandal had cost him his commission and he was making preparations to leave.

'Will you return, my lord?' Bessie ventured to ask.

A look of sadness and pain crossed his face but he gave a laugh and smiled down at her.

'To see those blue eyes and that lovely hair, of course I shall. Fare thee well, Bessie.'

Years passed. Often she would wonder where he was. There were rumours he was in Spain – or even more exotic climes. Other fine guests stayed at Cammells. Bessie drank in the atmosphere of culture and high living. One young scholar took a shine to her and taught her to read and write. She was a diligent student and she guessed he rather hoped she might be willing in other ways but she just bent her head over her books.

'One day I'll be as well read as any lady,' she thought. 'When my Lord Sandwich comes again, he will see how I've bettered myself, and then ...'

She didn't dare finish the thought, but the years ticked by and still she stayed at Cammells. By 1672 she was twenty-one, and most of her friends were married. Her parents worried that she had little time for any of the local lads. But Bessie was still waiting.

Once she had seen the great ships at anchor Bessie hurried back to the house to prepare for their lordships' arrival. They came when she was making up the earl's bed. As soon as she heard the carriage pull up she rushed to the window. For a long moment she gazed down at assembling lords, then she ran down to be in the hall to greet them with the rest of the household.

She bobbed a curtsey to the earl. He looked older, his face more lined and the curling brown hair streaked with grey. But in his brown eyes she read something that made her tremble. He tipped up her chin.

'Why, I do believe 'tis young Bessie, all grown up and passing fair.'

Bessie's feet hardly touched the ground. He remembered her!

The next few days passed in a whirl. The town was in high spirits. It was Whitsun and the taverns and alehouses were full of sailors. The shipwrights, rope-makers and victuallers were all working hard to ready the fleet for action. The house was abuzz with officers coming and going, the earl among them. But he always took time to speak to Bessie, and she dared to dream.

A council of war was called at Cammells on the evening of Whit Monday, 27 May. All the admirals and commanders were there. Bessie was kept busy serving drinks as the debate grew heated. She caught snatches as she bustled in and out.

'Your Highness, I urge you to put the fleet to sea without delay,' the earl was saying. 'We are sitting ducks here in the bay. The Dutch could be upon us at any time.'

'Nonsense, Montagu,' cried the duke. 'The Dutch are laid up at home. That little skirmish we had on the way up here sent them running. In any case, the wind is against them.'

'Your Highness, I insist that I do not think it prudent to remain at anchor. We need to muster the men as soon as possible.'

'"Insist", is it? May I remind you who is the superior officer here? Do you not keep allegiance to your king, my brother?'

The earl leapt to his feet, making Bessie jump and nearly spill the drink she was pouring. His kind, noble face was twisted in anger.

'Your Highness! I think only of our men, our ships, our country!'

With that the earl strode to the door. In the silence that followed, his feet could clearly be heard on the stairs. A door slammed overhead.

Bessie stood there, the ale jug shaking in her hand, till one of the officers waved her away. In the hallway Bessie hesitated a moment. Then, picking up her skirts, she ran up the stairs after him.

His face was grey when she opened the door.

'I – I've brought the ale, my lord. I thought perhaps ...'

'Oh, Bessie, you dear, sweet girl. You heard all that! 'Twas not for your ears.'

He beckoned her inside. Her heart began to thump.

'Whatever happens I shall do my duty,' he said. He was staring into space, and she guessed the words were not for her. 'I may not live to see the end of it. My dreams, lately, have warned me so.'

Bessie was aghast. 'O my lord, surely this can't be true!'

She stepped forward, her hands reaching out to him.

Bessie woke abruptly, hearing shouting and banging at the front door. The Dutch had been sighted. For a moment she didn't know where she was. Edward was stumbling from the bed and reaching for his clothes. Bessie hurried to help him. No words were said as he dressed. She noticed three rings lying by the bed and handed them to him. He slipped them into a pocket. She helped him into his breastplate, her fingers stumbling with the buckles as she thought of him going to war.

'Bessie, the sash.' He indicated the blue riband with the star and garter. She slipped it over his head and he adjusted it on his left shoulder so the medal hung on his right hip. She knew what it was, one of the highest honours in the land. He was ready to go, but now he turned back to Bessie.

'Farewell, my dear, kind and generous girl. You deserve more than this. Please forgive me.'

When he was gone, Bessie turned back to the tumbled bed and the clothes scattered on the floor. Numbly she bent and picked up one of his leather gloves that lay there forgotten, then, stifling her sobs, she ran to her attic room.

She didn't stay long. Once dressed, she flew out the door towards the sea. The night's peace was shattered by the beating of drums. There were officers and men-at-arms everywhere. As Bessie ran into the High Street people were spilling out and lamps were being lit. Carts rumbled over the cobbles, dogs barking, horses neighing, as soldiers, sailors and citizens surged down to the sea.

By half past five all ships were under sail. Many were woefully undermanned. Men who had gone to Dunwich, Aldeburgh and beyond for the holiday could not be reached in time. The townspeople gathered on the cliffs staring out to sea. The whole coastline seemed to shake from the noise of the guns as the battle raged just out of sight in the fog and smoke. All day the ships closed and fought, great bursts of flame showing where fire ships found their mark.

As news of the battle spread, more folk arrived to swell the crowd on the cliffs. Bessie listened to all the talk with her heart in her mouth. First, the English had the upper hand. Then word came the Dutch had the advantage. Invasion, once unimaginable, now seemed possible. Folk started to panic. The constable rallied the remaining seamen and some townsmen into a strong guard to prevent anyone from leaving.

'We must stand and defend ourselves against the foe!'

Anything that could be used as a weapon was marshalled and handed round.

But the invasion didn't happen. By six that evening the battle was over. No one really knew who was the victor, but they would sleep safe in their beds that night.

People began to go home, but Bessie lingered on the cliff, straining her eyes for any sign of a ship. It was not until the next day that the fleet began to limp home. Exhausted, Bessie watched them come. There was no sign of the *Royal James*. Cutters plied back and forth bringing the wounded ashore, and the little hospital on the green was soon full, but Bessie couldn't find Edward Montagu.

'The last I saw of the *James*,' a bandaged seaman rasped, 'she was ablaze from stem to stern. The first to fire on the Dutchies, she was, and fought bravely. God rest their souls.'

Bodies were washed on to the beaches for days afterwards. Whole and maimed, friend and foe, shreds of clothing streaming like seaweed on the shingle. Bessie was there at every tide, desperately searching, her hair bedraggled, her dress stained with salt. She had to know if he had died, so she turned over corpse after grisly corpse.

At the house, her fellow servants tried to stop her, make her sleep, eat. But she could not. They suggested she go home to her family but she would not leave. In Edward's room she smoothed the bedcover over and over. Every time there was someone at the door she peered from the window, hoping it was him.

Word came at last two weeks after the battle. The earl's body had been recovered off the coast of Essex, identifiable only by his star and garter sash and the three rings in his pocket.

On hearing the news, Bessie sank to her knees with a moan. After a time she went slowly up the stairs. Next morning she couldn't be found; her attic room had not been slept in. It was only when another maid went into the earl's chamber that Bessie was found. She was lying on the bed, a man's leather glove clasped in her cold dead hands.

Edward Montagu was given a state funeral, his body brought up the Thames in a flotilla of barges. Bessie's own funeral was much simpler, and her spirit lingers in the house to this day. In Sutherland House, as it's now known, her footsteps trip lightly between the attic and the earl's bedchamber, where the bedclothes can be found disturbed even when no one has slept there. On 28 May, the anniversary of the Battle of Sole Bay, her pale face may be seen at an upstairs window, her red hair and blue eyes catching the light as she waits for her lord to return.

8

The Secret Burial

Many decades had passed since I had been to Great Livermere. The boy I had been had disappeared as surely as the place I remembered. I'd heard that they'd knocked the Hall down twenty years ago, back in '23, but I will confess it was a shock to see the mere stretching out without that grimy white façade behind it. My guide, a young man deputised from the local hostelry to see me safely to the mere, reminisced that he and the other boys had sneaked into the surviving underground kitchens and had found a tunnel that led them almost to the water. I remembered the teas that used to come out of those kitchens, muffins dripping with butter, fruit cake heady with brandy, and the iced buns that I and my friend preferred.

The path up to the mere was still good, but at my age any walk is rather a slog. We were going so slowly that I could hear the cries of water birds undisturbed by our creaking approach. I have always found their calls to be eerie, haunting sounds, but today they seemed especially full of melancholy. I was not insensible to the fact that this matched my mood. As we inched on I was rewarded with my first glimpse of St Peter and St Paul's across the water, the tall tower rising up from the elder trees. Looking back towards The Rectory, I saw the plantation, a few dark, exotic trees marking its presence behind new, young hawthorns. As I stared, a dark shape shot up from the trees.

My guide took my arm as I stumbled, and together we watched the crow race across the water.

'It's a crying shame it's got so overgrown and forgotten. The war'll make it worse, o' course.'

'It will make a lot of things worse, young man.' I was glad that my old friend hadn't lived to see our country descend once more into war. But there are many wars, even ones we fight with ourselves, so modern psychoanalysis tells us. Wars inside that can change a boy from one meeting to the next.

I was just an occasional visitor at Livermere Hall in those long-ago days of the late 1860s. I looked forward to our visits as chance to get away from the town and to race around as boys like to do. My friend was a cousin of the owner, and, being much the same age, we were introduced in the expectation of our getting on, and him getting me out of the house. We became friends in the manner of small boys, delighting in the long sunlit days spent climbing trees, examining frogspawn and stealing birds' eggs.

The day it happened was to be the last that he and I would see each other that summer. We were both due to go off to our prep schools for the first time, and the tea that had been provided was particularly lavish. I retired to bed that night with an aching belly, and the next day my parents and I travelled back to Bury not knowing that anything was amiss.

When we met again the next summer we were both changed. My friend spoke incessantly of ghosts and secrets and ghastly histories. School had made me more nervous, and this talk scared me. That visit would be our last meeting as children, for my parents moved away from Suffolk and we never returned to the Hall. Sometimes I would look back on those golden summer days with wistfulness, but my friend's strange stories had coloured the memories for me and I made no attempt to keep in touch.

It was many years later when we met once more, quite by chance. It was during the last war. I had some work in Cambridge, and we met on the street. I recognised him straight away – he seemed little changed despite the decades that had passed. After our exclamations of pleasure, I fully expected him to go on his way, but instead he invited me back to his rooms in the college where he worked. Beneath high ceilings and tall windows, I was treated to supper and sherry.

Our reminiscences drew long into the evening, and after a few sherries I felt emboldened to mention the change I had perceived come over him, so long ago.

He sighed, poured us both another brimming glass of sherry and began his tale.

It had happened the very day we'd parted. We'd been solemn that day, realising that we were getting quite grown up and that our lives were changing. These things, he said, were on his mind as he made his way to the bridge over the mere. He was glad, therefore, to encounter a villager making his way back too, and they chatted until the time came for my friend to head along the path to the plantation, and thence home. He waved goodbye to the villager and started off, but after a few yards something made him look back. To his surprise, the man was still standing there, staring into the trees as if transfixed. Seeing my friend looking, the man doffed his cap and went on his way, but my friend felt the first thread of unease run up his spine.

We had spent many happy hours in the plantation, but now, as the dusk came on, those trees seemed not the old friends they had always been. As my friend walked on he felt a prickling at the back of his neck. Turning, he half expected to see the villager, but there were only the straight dark shapes of the trees and the long shadows across the bare ground. On he went, but he was sure there was something, some faint noise behind him. He whirled around again – and at the corner of his vision it seemed to him that he saw a pale shape extract itself from the shadows and flit across the trees. In that long moment of clarity, he was sure he saw a shrouded figure in the shape of a man.

The next instant, it was gone. My friend ran until he reached the wooden gate to The Rectory, his home. He fastened it with unusual care and ran for the house.

His nursery faced the plantation, and he felt a creeping dread of the night come over him and entreated his nurse to stay, telling her of his vision in the wood.

The nurse was unsympathetic. 'The idea of the thing!' she cried. 'I'll not have such unnatural talk in my nursery!'

Sleep was elusive. Long after the sun had set and the house had gone quiet, he arose from his bed and stared out across the garden to the dark trees.

In the morning he wasn't sure if he had seen anything, but he elected to stay in, even though the day was bright. It did no good. That night he had a terrible dream. He was walking, as a grown man, it seemed, through a dark churchyard. The moon was high, and he glimpsed a gravestone with a white death's head. He wasn't alone, but his companion walked ahead. He felt a sick anticipation and pressed a whistle to his mouth and blew. Then a dark shape leapt from the shadows and set upon his companion. A deep feeling of satisfaction settled on him as his companion was borne to the ground …

He awoke screaming. His nurse was solicitous, and his mother came and sat by his bed. At length they left him drowsy with hot milk, and he heard his mother whisper, '… must be the thought of school. Oh, I do worry we send them away too young!'

The dreams returned all summer, and he couldn't lose the sensation that something was out there, in the trees. He asked the villagers, but his concerns were dismissed as fancies. Nonetheless, he detected in their denials something that made him surer of what he'd seen.

Then, as he was playing in the garden on one of the last days of summer, the light changed. All the colour of the day was gone, and as he looked up he realised that he was alone. Something drew his attention to the wooden gate to the plantation. He saw, with, he said, a punch to the diaphragm, a flash of white behind the latch. Unable to stop himself, he crept to the gate and peered through. Looking back at him from the other side was a face. It was a hot face, angry-seeming, but he was sure it was no living man who stared at him, the whites all visible round the eyes, a flutter of drapery at the brow.

My friend bolted for the house. He was deeply glad that the last few days before he went to school were wet. He was sure he would never forget, but in the homesickness and bustle of those early days away, the incident soon went from his mind. However, on his returning home for Christmas and seeing the gate once more, it all came back.

When an outing to the Hall was proposed, his heart sank, but with his brothers and sister beside him, and the plantation bright under the bare trees, all was well. It was only him and his sister on the way home, his elder brothers being allowed to stay up after dark. He was sure he would be safe with her beside him, but as they came to the plantation path she waved him goodbye and ran off to see a friend in one of the gatehouse cottages. After no more than a term of school he was already

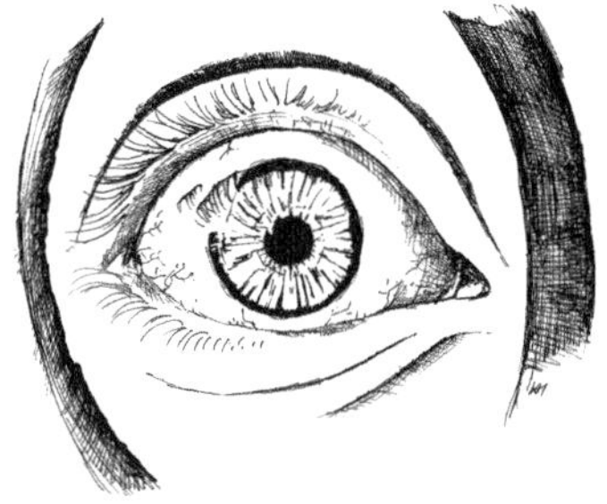

too proud either to beg her to stay or to run after her. With a heavy heart, into the plantation he trudged.

It was late in the afternoon. The darkness of the trees closed over him and he was immediately conscious of a rustling. It seemed that each step he took had an echo, speeding up as he did. He made it to the gate, but as he went to open it something brushed against him and, without thinking, he turned. Right behind him stood the grinning figure, a dirty white cloth flapping around its ghastly form.

The dreams returned after that. His refusals to go to the Hall were tolerated because he seemed so ill. But, when it came to New Year, he was told he must go to the party, that it would do him good. He felt like one condemned until he was told that the carriage was to be used.

It was a jolly occasion, and the younger members of the party played game after game. They rambled over the house, into rooms not then used, and in the melee, my friend knocked against a desk in a dusty study and bucketed yellowing papers to the floor.

'I'll just put these back,' he called, and bent to gather them.

As he did, one piece floated free. In reaching out to snatch it, he felt a shiver run through him, and the rest fell once more to the floor. With trembling fingers he began to read. The writing was hard for such a young boy, but he was able to pick it out.

The paper told of a trial more than 150 years before, in 1721, of Arundell Coke, a former owner of the Hall. Falling on hard times through hard living, he had sold it and moved to Bury, but schemed to get it back. His hopes lay in his sister's husband's riches. This Mr

Crisp, when he died, had willed everything to Coke's sister, and Coke was her executor … A plan was formed, the services of a certain John Woodbourne were contracted, and, late one night as Coke walked his brother-in-law home across the churchyard, Woodbourne attacked, and they left Crisp for dead.

With a jolt my friend remembered his dream, but nothing would have stopped him reading on.

Crisp lived to tell his tale, and Coke and Woodbourne were arrested for his maiming. Coke tried to cheat the hangman by twisting the law to say that, since he had planned murder, not maiming, they could not condemn them on that accusation. Justice won and the two were hanged.

Thus ended the printed epistle, but in a shaky hand someone had written, 'in the trees?', and then under that, in firmer letters, 'secret burial'.

My friend could hardly believe what he had read. Quickly folding the paper, he stuffed it in his pocket.

The next day saw him at the church, pestering the old warden whether he knew of any secret burials, or of the Coke family. The old man stared at the boy a long while, then led him inside. He beckoned him into the chancel, and when my friend followed he found he was staring straight at a skull!

It was just part of the memorial, but it took him a moment to calm down. The memorial was for a Richard Coke, his wife, and the baby daughter of, yes, Arundell Coke. But not Arundell himself.

'They say they snuck him back from Bury and buried him right here,' said the warden. 'But thas just an old tale. Maybe they did, but – a murderer, in the church? I reckon he's buried out there.' He jerked his thumb out towards the plantation. 'And good riddance!'

My friend went home thoughtful that day.

'I never saw or felt anything there again,' he said as we sipped yet another sherry. 'It was as if my knowing his history was enough to quiet him. But I'll never forget the self-satisfied malice I felt from him.'

'You must write it down,' I urged, but my friend brushed my words away.

I never saw him again after that, and was saddened to hear of his death four years ago. However, when I heard that a new story had been published after his death, one that pertained to his own life, I rushed out as fast as my old bones would let me to buy a copy.

The story I read wasn't what he had told me. There were elements, certainly, but … I must confess I was disappointed.

As I looked around at plantation and mere, it seemed to me that the place had an undeniable feel of menace, one that I hadn't sensed a moment before. I wrenched my mind from the past and turned to my guide.

'Are there any ghosts here, do you know?'

The man laughed.

'Ghosts? We're the most haunted village in Suffolk! Why, just here by the church and mere there's a grey lady, a lad on a bicycle and a man on a penny-farthing.' He gestured towards the bridge. 'Someone saw an old man in the reeds there. Plenty more in the village, too, they say.'

I had to laugh. All those sightings, but not a hint of the presence my friend had seen, and had failed to speak of in that published story. Well, the tale was mine now, and, as I'm no writer, I suppose it will die with me.

9

A Gift from the Sea

Things were simpler back when I was a lad. Harder, perhaps, but simpler. Our little fishing hamlet didn't seem much affected by the twentieth century. The long shingle beach and the sand dunes fringed with marram were broken only by the ragged lines of concrete sea defences from the last war. We thought them like giants' broken teeth. The beach was our playground, along with the heathland and woods behind.

Mum, Dad and me, we lived in one of the coastguard cottages up on the cliff. Built by the navy over a hundred years ago they were, a defence against the smugglers. There were no smugglers by our day, least not as we knew. Nan and Grandpa lived in the row of houses beside the road. Grandpa'd been a fisherman all his life. By then there wasn't much call for such small-scale fishing, so Dad had a job at the engineering works in town – but at weekends he'd help Grandpa on his boat.

We kids would run down to the foreshore in the early morning light, through the horned poppies and sea kale, to see what the boats were bringing in. We never thought about the hard work. For us it was all about the catch. Cod, plaice, herring, lobster, crab – or the shrimps we loved best, boiled up in Grandpa's black shed, sweet and delicious. There were never enough!

That day, I was at Grandpa's elbow as he stirred the pot, half listening to his usual grumps about the small catch. I was really just waiting for my cupful to take home.

Then Grandpa exclaimed, 'Well, blas' me, bor! How did that git in thar?'

My attention caught, I peered into the boiling pot. There, bobbing about among the shrimps, was a huge red lobster.

'Blas' me!' said Grandpa. 'I never seed him afore.'

'And you won't see his like again.'

Grandpa and I spun round, fair frit out of our skins.

In the doorway to the shed stood a man. He looked just an ordinary fisherman in his blue trousers and gansey. He had a thick, curly beard and a cap pushed back on his head. I'd never seen him before, and Grandpa looked as puzzled as me.

'And who might you be a-telling me I won't be seeing another lobster?' said Grandpa.

The stranger gave him a long, slow smile. 'That's no lobster you've got there. You'll find that's a shrimp.'

Grandpa bristled, and I was sure he was going to chuck the stranger out, but then he looked into the pot again.

Carefully fishing the creature out of the pot, he cried, 'Well, I'll be! You'm right, bor. It is, it's a bloomin' grut shrimp!'

The stranger's smile reached his eyes. Strange eyes, they were, shifting and changing with the sound of the waves, first blue, then green, then grey.

'You can keep him. As long as you have him your shrimping nets will be full.'

Grandpa humphed at that. 'Thas a big promise. Just who did you say you were?'

The stranger leant forward and whispered in Grandpa's ear. As he did, the salty tang of the sea, always pretty strong inside the shed, swelled so much that I fell back, dizzy. Grandpa's eyes were popping, but his next words were calm: 'If you say so, bor. I'll find summat to put him in and we'll see, we'll see.' Then, turning to me: 'Fetch me that old tin. That'll do for it.'

I grabbed the tin, and in went the Grut Shrimp. We stowed the tin on a shelf. When we turned round we were alone. No trace of the stranger save a lingering tang of salty air.

Next night, Dad and Grandpa took the boat out, and I saw Grandpa stash the Shrimp's tin on board.

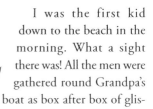

I was the first kid down to the beach in the morning. What a sight there was! All the men were gathered round Grandpa's boat as box after box of glistening brown shrimps was hauled off the deck. None of the other boats had a catch like that.

'Just struck lucky,' Grandpa said.

He looked troubled, though, as he gazed out to sea. I was sure he wasn't exactly telling the truth. I was sure it was something to do with what the stranger had whispered, but I didn't dare ask.

Grandpa's luck – or whatever it was – held. All through the shrimping season that year his catches were huge. Years later, Dad told me that some folk were muttering against Grandpa. Why should he have all the luck?

Come the end of the shrimp season, when the fishermen moved on to the next catch, spring herring, his hauls were much the same as everyone else's, and everyone relaxed. The next year, though, same thing happened again. With the tin and its fishy cargo stowed on board, the shrimps filled Grandpa's nets to bursting.

He'd always been a good'un, my grandpa. He taught me that all true fishermen respect the sea. He was always careful, never taking out of season, and he argued with the other fishermen against taking too much from the sea.

'You have to give in order to git,' he'd say.

As for me, the day of the Grut Shrimp had given me a fascination with the creatures of the sea. As soon as I was big enough I'd go out with Grandpa. He needed all the help he could get in shrimp season! We were all night hauling and filling them boxes. The tin always went out with him. I remember suggesting once that we should leave it behind, as an experiment, but Grandpa wouldn't hear of it.

Then everything changed. No one much used to come here. A few holiday-makers, perhaps, and locals from Leiston and the like to enjoy the beach and sand dunes. A kiosk selling sweets and soft drinks opened up in summer, but that was it. Who'd've guessed we'd soon be on the map?

The plans for the power station were public knowledge by 1960. Aged eleven, I thought it sounded exciting. I wasn't the only one.

People'd say, 'Think of all the jobs!' and, 'We'll get the electric now, 'bout time.'

Some folks got up a petition against it, but the small man doesn't stand a chance against the big boys, does he? Within a year the land just north of the village was a building site. To us kids it was an adventure playground in the early days when security was, to say the least, haphazard.

The boats still put to sea, but there were fewer every year. Grandpa carried on, with Dad's help and mine. Still the shrimps were his star catch. Sometimes I'd sneak a peek at the Grut Shrimp. Just a shell now, but it was still Grandpa's lucky charm.

I'd gone away to college by the time the power station was up and running. By then I was keen to leave village life behind. I had my sights set on science. I was going to be a marine biologist. Because of that shrimp, I suppose.

I still came home in the holidays. Grandpa was slowing down. He'd stopped everything save the shrimps. He was always around the few other boats, though, yarning with his mates, mending pots and nets and pottering in his shed. I'd walk with him of an evening along the shore. He'd stop with his back to the grey hulk of the power station and stare out to sea, hands in pockets, lost in thoughts he'd never share.

When he was too frail to carry on fishing and the boat fell to Dad to use, Grandpa put the Grut Shrimp's tin away on its shelf in the shed. No one else dared touch it. He never did tell me what the stranger'd said all those years ago.

I came home when Dad sent word that Grandpa didn't have long. I sat with him and listened while he yarned about the old days.

'Bring me my old tin, bor,' he whispered. 'Thas bin along o' me a good while, and I'd have it with me now.'

When I placed it in his hands, the room suddenly filled with the smell of the sea. I looked around and there, standing in the doorway, was the stranger. It'd been many years since I'd seen him in Grandpa's shed, but he was unchanged. Same blue trousers and gansey, same cap on his head, his beard still curly and dark. The hairs on my neck prickled and my mouth went dry.

He smiled that long, slow smile.

'A true son of the sea, your grandfather. He has served us well. He was well deserving of the gift. There's not many who are.'

I heard a sound beside me – and turned to see that Grandpa had slipped away. There was a peaceful smile on his face.

I wrenched my attention back to the stranger.

'Who are you?' I whispered.

There was a sudden roar as if a huge wave was coming in. My hands leapt up to protect myself. The stranger's figure seemed to waver, then he was gone.

I staggered up to the door but there was no one there, just that lingering tang of the sea. Returning to the bed, I lifted the tin from Grandpa's unresisting hands and opened the lid. The Grut Shrimp's shell was gone. In its place lay a shard of driftwood – in the shape of a trident.

The evening after Grandpa's funeral I walked along the shore as I'd done with him so many times. As darkness fell I stood with my back to the power station and looked out to sea. Although there was only a sliver of moon the sea was shimmering and glistening. I walked down to the water's edge and saw, dancing under the surface, a mass of tiny shrimps glowing like little lamps in the sea. I waded in to try and catch some but they darted out of reach. I stood entranced among them, and then I saw, in the midst of them, one huge shrimp. There were rumours, those days, about what the power station was doing to the local sea life, but I knew what this was. As I watched, the shrimps began to drift away from the shore in a luminescent stream. A warm feeling of understanding filled me. I lifted my hand to wave to the shrimps – and that one special one – and a burst of shooting stars leapt across the sky.

'Bye, Grandpa,' I said. 'I'll carry on your care of the sea.'

10

The Mistletoe Bride

Amy loved the Tudors. They'd done them at school and got to dress up like a Tudor and cook like a Tudor and everything. Her mum got her a book of stories from Shakespeare. Amy read them over and over. They'd been to Framlingham Castle and gone up on the train to Ipswich to see Christchurch Mansion, but when Amy saw a leaflet advertising Tudor Days at Kentwell Hall that summer she couldn't believe her eyes. She pestered her mum until she agreed they could go for the whole weekend.

When they got there, Amy was so excited. The house was just like on the posters, with a turret and a moat and everything. It was the perfect Tudor house. Everywhere she looked were people dressed up, and she could hear Tudor music. She wanted to experience it all at once.

Her mum insisted they stick together, even though Amy wanted to see the Tudor kitchen in the old hall and her brothers wanted to see the cannons. There was a lot of complaining when she dragged them to the kitchen. She begged her mum to be left there for a bit. She was ten now: big enough to look after herself. Her mum looked worried, but then Jamie knocked over a bowl of flour. The re-enactor looked like she wanted to try some proper Tudor punishment on him.

Her mum gave in. 'You be careful now. Don't go too far – and don't leave the grounds! Don't talk to strangers!'

She said she'd be back in an hour, but Amy didn't care – you could do a lot of exploring in an hour! She waited a few minutes after her mum had gone, and then, while a new family were talking to the re-enactors, she darted out into the gardens.

Everything was in full bloom. Amy was enchanted. She walked along by the fish pond, imagining herself a fine lady, swishing past in stiff skirts. At the end were greenhouses, with boringly twentieth-century-looking gardeners pottering about. Next to the greenhouses was a gateway, so through it Amy slipped. A reedy stream and a shed full of pots. Boring. Out through the next gate she came – there ahead of her was a long sunken hollow of grass, and, sitting at the top of it, a girl her own age.

Shyly, Amy approached. The girl was dressed strangely, in what appeared to be a long, embroidered white nightgown.

'Hello, I'm Amy. Are you with the re-enactors?'

The girl jumped up. 'No, I live here.'

Amy doubted that, but allowed it as she'd been playing make-believe, too.

They played together, rolling down the slope and climbing back up again until Amy almost felt sick with laughing. There was an odd moment when she asked the other girl's name. The girl's face darkened and she turned away. But Amy soon forgot about that.

When they'd exhausted themselves and flopped down at the top of the slope, Amy decided to test her new friend by asking her about living there. The girl gave strange answers that couldn't be true, talking about servants and carriage journeys and governesses. Amy smiled. Make-believe was fun! She asked if there were any stories about the hall.

'I do know one. It's a ghost story. Are you brave enough?'

Stung, Amy said that she was.

'It happened long ago,' said the girl. 'Mama said it was in the Tudor times you like so much, when the hall was new. It was Christmas time, she said, and the snow lay thick upon the ground, but even though people don't usually travel in the snow, there was a party at the hall because the lord's daughter was getting married!

'The wedding was on Christmas Day. There were games and dancing, but as the day wore on, the bride, who was called Ginevra, started to get nervous about the wedding night.'

The two girls giggled.

'She liked her husband, Lovell,' the girl went on. 'He was handsome and seemed kind, and he had given her a ruby ring, but she hardly knew him. The more she thought about it, the more nervous she got. So, when she saw people starting to yawn she jumped up.

'"Let's have one more game before we sleep! Let's play hide and seek!"

'Everyone looked at Lovell, but he was laughing.

'"Very well, my bride. We will play, but on one condition." He pointed up at the mistletoe above his head. "Give me a kiss under the mistletoe, and then we will seek you, my lovely bride."

'Blushing, Ginevra stepped over to Lovell and raised her mouth for a kiss.'

The girls giggled again, but Amy's friend was soon serious. 'Lovell thought his bride had never looked lovelier, with her long yellow hair maiden-loose for the last time, her white silk dress flowing around her. He pulled down a bit of the mistletoe and garlanded her head with it.

'"So I may find you all the more easily, the mistletoe will call you to me," he whispered.

'Ginevra didn't know what to say to that, so out of the hall she ran to hide.

'The guests began the search, but Ginevra must have found a good hiding place, because they couldn't find her. At first the searching was done with laughter and gaiety, but after an hour Lovell and Ginevra's father began to feel afraid. Everyone searched, servants and guests alike. They turned the house upside down, but Ginevra couldn't be found.

'Her father feared she had run away for fear of the wedding night. He ordered the servants to search outside, but the snow was still falling. Any tracks she might have left had disappeared. In the morning, Lovell and the lord sent out riders to the village, and to all the halls nearby, but nothing was found.

'Eventually they had to give up, but for many months Lovell hoped to hear that Ginevra had been found. All he could think of was her sweet face looking up at him moments before she had run away.

'His friends told him he should remarry, but he never did. His servants whispered that Ginevra must have been a fairy-bride. She'd ensorcelled him with her charms, they said, and then gone back to her fairy-world, leaving him lost and alone.

'One day, many years after that fateful day, he went back to Kentwell. The new lord welcomed him, but while they were sitting sharing a drink by the fire a servant rushed into the room.

'"My lords, you must come!"

'They hurried after the servant, following her up into the attics. Lovell remembered the attics from that dreadful night, but he was sure he'd never been in this dusty room. A group of servants were standing around an open chest, their faces stricken.

'"We thought this chest was locked, my lords, so we dusted it and carried on, but then Sukey knocked against it as she swept the floor, and it sprung open. And – well, you best see for yourselves, my lords."

'The new lord stepped forward and peered into the chest. What he saw made him gasp and step back.

'"Lovell," he said. "You'd better come and see."

'Lovell suddenly knew what he would see. There, in the chest, lay a skeleton. It still had long yellow hair, and there were shreds of white cloth over it, and, coiled in the hair, he could see the yellowed strands of some leafy plant, with shrivelled brown berries.'

'He knew, but he had to be sure. Leaning in, he saw that on the corpse's hand was a ring – a ring he recognised, a ruby ring! It was

Ginevra! She must have crept into the attics, pulled the lid down too hard and locked herself in. Why had they not searched all the chests?

'With trembling hands Lovell reached out and touched the golden hair, but it crumpled to dust at his touch.'

'That's horrid!' cried Amy, clapping her hands over her ears.

'But that's not all,' crowed the other girl. 'My mama used to sing me the story when I was little, and she told me that after they opened the chest they let Ginevra's spirit out – and she's still here, haunting the hall! Look!' she cried, pointing at one of the upper windows at the back of the house. 'There she is now! Can't you see her face?'

Amy looked. Sure enough there was someone looking straight back at her, with pale hair tumbling round her face.

'I don't want to hear any more of your stupid stories,' she cried, and away she ran.

She didn't say anything about the girl or her story to her mum when they met up again, but stayed close to her and her brothers. The next day, she wasn't really sure that she wanted to go, but when they arrived everything looked so much fun that she was excited once more. Her mum said she could go off on her own again, as she'd been such a good girl the day before.

Her feet took her back into the gardens where she made herself look up at the window. There was no one there. But at the back of the gardens she saw her friend, jumping up and waving at her, with a big smile on her face. At the sight of the smile, Amy forgave her and ran over to play.

The two girls played for most of the day, making believe they were fine ladies. No mention was made of the story.

When Amy went back to her mum at teatime she was full of stories of her new friend.

'What a nice little girl,' said Mum. 'We should go and thank her mother for letting her play, don't you think?'

So they trooped back to the garden. Mum asked the gardeners if they'd seen where the girl had gone. The gardeners looked baffled.

'Amy's been here most of the day,' said a young, red-haired woman. 'But there wasn't another girl. She's been playing by herself. Such an imaginative child!'

Amy couldn't believe her ears, but because she didn't know the girl's name her mum wouldn't believe there'd been a girl at all. She said that Amy had made it all up. There was nothing Amy could do to persuade her otherwise.

Amy didn't go back to Kentwell for many years. But, when she was a student, some of her friends visited her in the holidays, and, being history students, they were keen to see Suffolk's stately homes. She felt a stab of unease when Kentwell was suggested, but everyone else was keen.

Those two strange days were foremost in her mind as they walked around the grounds. She began to tell her friends about the ghost story and her imaginary friend.

'O Amy,' they cried. 'You're so silly!'

'Amy?'

One of the gardeners stood beside them, a red-haired woman in her thirties.

'Are you really Amy?' she said.

Amy was unsettled, but she nodded.

'I remember you,' said the gardener. 'It must've been ten years ago, but we all remember. You were playing all alone. But the next day, after you were gone, we heard a child's voice in the garden, calling out your name, over and over. But whenever we looked, there was no one there. Every year we hear that voice, calling, "Amy, Amy", and we wondered – were you telling the truth, after all, about your little friend?'

Amy stared at her, hardly believing what she'd heard. All the emotions from all those years ago came rushing back and she had to turn away. She stared blankly into the gardens, and there, on the slope, she saw a little girl, dressed in a white nightgown, waving and waving as if she'd seen an old friend.

11

If You Go into the Woods

For more than forty years the desiccating body of Jonah Snell hung in chains on the gibbet in Potsford Wood. Since 1699, it had swung in the breeze as a reminder of his crimes. By 1740 most who walked past had forgotten who he was and why he was there. The people who went to and from Wickham Market averted their gaze from the dangling bones and rusting chains and scurried quickly by.

One day, a tailor by the name of James Gall was on his way to Letheringham. Gall prided himself on being a rationalist, a free thinker unbound by the superstitions of his age – whether those of the church or of the folk. He passed by that way often enough, and Snell's grinning skull was like an old friend.

That morning, feeling a sprite of mischief inside him, Gall greeted the gristly brown bones: 'Aha, old fellow, it would be a strange thing if thou were to come down from there.'

Chuckling to himself, he continued on his way and thought no more about it until, job done, he was on his way home again. It was dusk by then, the trees shrouded in shadow. Gall's thoughts were not on the darkening wood but on the miller's suit he was to make. When he came to the corner where the gibbet stood, though, he glanced up, still thinking of the mill.

He stopped dead. For there, where this morning had hung the chain-bound brown bones, was nothing but an empty hook.

Gall remembered he was a rationalist and, with a shaky laugh, he said, 'Hast thou chosen this day of all days to be laid to thy long deservéd rest? Have they taken thee down and buried thee?'

Sure that that was the explanation, Gall turned to go – only to freeze when he heard, right behind him, a clink, a sharp metallic chink. It was a familiar sound to anyone who walked through Potsford Wood; the sound of metal touching metal, of Jonah Snell's chains shifting in the breeze.

But Jonah Snell was no longer on his gibbet.

Rationalism offered no answers, but Gall's feet knew what to do. He ran.

Clink, clank, clank came the sound of chains behind him.

No matter how fast he ran, the clanking matched his pace. Clink, clank, clink, clank. He told himself he didn't believe in ghosts, but he didn't look behind him as he ran. Close to the edge of the wood he was, yet still behind him came the clank, clank, clank, faster and faster, until at last Gall sprinted into the open fields, and he didn't stop running until he was home.

That Sunday, James Gall found a spot in the pew closest to the pulpit and listened to the vicar with a rapt expression and his prayer book clutched to his chest.

As it happens, it was later that year that they took Snell down and buried his brown bones in the wood. But by then it was too late. Something had stirred that no burial could allay. The wood became a colder place. His presence drifted, nothing but formless anger and the sharp memory of blood. When people walked through the wood now, they shivered as they came to the spot where the gibbet once had been; they drew their collars up around their necks and hurried on.

Scraps of memory came to the spirit. The dry dusty scent of flour. The solid heft of a maul. The taste of brandy. Blood, so much blood. And anger.

Time went on, more memories formed. He'd been a journeyman: all the skills of a master, but none of the respect – and none of the money.

He could see the mill at Letheringham. Remembered the father and son counting money. The anger burned.

'Kill them now!' the devil voice in his head had whispered. 'Make them pay!'

Lifting the maul. Blood spurting everywhere, obliterating the miller's accounts, pooling around the coins, soaking through the floor, dripping into the flour sacks below.

He'd hauled the bodies up and strung them upside down to bleed from a beam.

'That's right,' whispered the voice. 'They're going straight down to hell.'

Then out he'd walked into the sunshine, blinking at the brightness, the metallic scent of blood following him as he walked away down the river while the birds sang.

'The Devil made me do it,' he'd said in the courtroom at Wickham Market.

The feel of the rough rope around his neck, the jeering crowds in the marketplace, the sudden crushing pain …

Then this wood, this track and the anger never ceasing.

The gibbet post rotted as the seasons turned, collapsing into the undergrowth, the story forgotten, and the presence drifted, angry, confused, lost … stretched so thin that there was almost nothing left.

In 1958 men clearing scrub in the wood uncovered the post. Dusty old records were consulted, Snell's story uncovered. The post was raised, railings commissioned and a plaque affixed to the post commemorating Snell – the last person hanged at Wickham Market. People came to see and the quiet wood was, for a while, alive with voices.

Something heard. *Jonah Snell, Jonah Snell.* That was him, that was *him*. In the silent wood the birds leapt from their roosts and flew, squawking, into the sky, and the leaf litter whirled around the railings.

The gamekeeper working in the wood stopped and stared around, then shrugged. Who knew what scared birds?

'Them fast motor vehicles on the road, most likely,' he thought, noting that, though there was an hour of daylight left, he could already see the headlights.

'Strange though,' he muttered. 'Thas surely coming from the other side of the wood.'

Picking up his gun in case there were intruders, he made his way towards the track and emerged out by the gibbet corner. The rotten old post stood within its crisp black railings, the last of the afternoon's sun bright upon it. There was no one to be seen. He shook his head, and was turning to go when suddenly he felt an icy touch on his shoulder.

'Who's there?' he cried.

In silence the presence answered: *Jonah Snell, Jonah Snell.*

Up flew the birds.

Spooked, the gamekeeper legged it. In the pub that night he swore blind that as he'd run he'd heard the clanking of chains.

People trod more softly in the wood after that. They whispered how there was a stone that screamed if you stood on it, *that's* where he was buried, they said, and the presence coiled around them so that they pulled up their collars and shivered.

A lorry driver, caught short, pulled up and wandered up the track. His need relieved, he spotted the railed post up ahead and, curious, sauntered over to look.

'Last known hanging 14 April 1699, Jonah Snell,' he read.

The presence came like a bloodhound on the scent. An icy hand descended on the lorry driver's shoulder. The man wheeled about, and there, staring back at him, was a hooded figure, its face no more than a grinning brown skull.

With a yell the lorry driver ran out of the wood, leapt into his cab and sped away, swearing he'd never take a slash in the woods again.

The presence rejoiced in the man's fear, remembering how good the miller and his son's fear had felt on that day long ago. Lights flickered on and off in the wood, hardly visible in the sunshine.

It was late one night when the couple's car broke down. With no choice but to get out and find the nearest house or phone box, they set off up Dragarse Hill. As they passed the wood Jenny saw a light.

'There must be a house up there,' she said. 'See – there's a track.'

'You'd need a 4x4 to get up there,' muttered Matt.

'Got any better options?' came the tart reply.

Into the wood they went. Their torch flashed up and down the trees, shadows looming out at them. They jumped at every sound. Was there something chinking in the wind? Wind chimes, maybe? Except there was no wind.

'Is it me,' whispered Matt, 'or is that light moving?'

They rounded a bend and right ahead, stark in the torchlight, was a tall, ragged post and spiky rails.

'What's that?' cried Jenny. Fear pooled off them both and spilled into the wood.

As they stood there rooted to the spot, a dark shape moved across the narrow beam of light from their torch. Getting closer …

They ran, and behind them there came the chink, clank, clank of chains …

As they raced back up the road the presence floated on the edge of his demesne and laughed.

There were those, however, who used the wood at night for their own means, and no ghost was going to put them off. Bob regularly went into Potsford Wood to check his snares. Nothing had ever happened to him, despite the stories people told. He doffed his cap at the gibbet as he passed each night, and that was enough for him.

That night the moon was high and headlights from the cars flashed by as Bob went round his snares. Soon enough he had a brace of rabbits for the pot. He was satisfied with the night's work. Rabbits stuffed in his bag, he headed back home, his path going out on to the track the better to walk in the moonlight.

He was just about to tap his cap at the gibbet when he realised he was no longer alone. Clustered around the gibbet was a group of pale figures. Bob's first thought was that they were gamekeepers, but the figures stood silent and still.

Had Snell brought his ghostly friends to the wood? Bob didn't stop to find out. He turned tail and ran.

He awoke the next morning to the memory of those figures. In the grey light of day he chided himself for being foolish. Before he knew what he was doing, his boots were back on and he was heading back up the track. It was a grey, misty morning, silent as the grave.

'Roight, in yew go,' he muttered as he reached the wood.

In the mist the figures loomed. Bob nearly turned and ran again, but there was something about those figures … steeling himself, he crept closer. Then he burst out laughing.

'Thas play'n silly buggers!' he cried.

For there were no ghosts floating dead and drear around the gibbet post, only garden statues!

He laughed all the way back home, calling himself a duzzy old fool! He couldn't for the life of him think what they were doing there. Was it an April Fool? It wasn't until he saw the news headline about the garden centre theft that he put two and two together and alerted the authorities.

In the wood, if there had been anyone to see, they'd have seen a dark shape drifting around the fauns and naked goddesses. The presence revelled in his night's work. The look on the faces of the thieves sneaking through the wood with their plunder. The shock and fear – like on the faces of John Bullard and his son as he raised the maul so long ago. They'd all remember Jonah Snell.

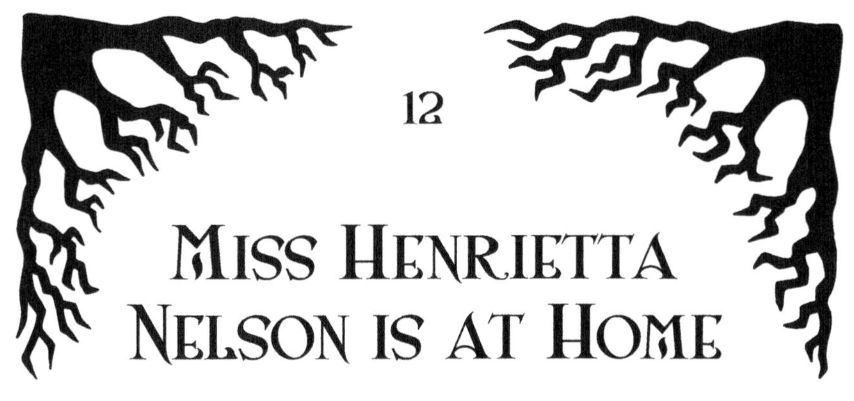

12

Miss Henrietta Nelson is at Home

Henrietta enjoyed the weddings at Yaxley Hall. After the excitement of returning home she watched all the comings and goings with delight. She didn't quite understand why people were paying to be married here, but, no matter, it was fun.

From her position in the entrance hall she greeted the guests with a smile, relishing the sight of smartly dressed people flowing into the house. Sometimes she'd slip into the gardens and mingle with the guests on the lawns. She couldn't resist the temptation: the tented pavilions and flower-decked tables were so beautiful. If anyone caught a glimpse of a lady of mature years in a long blue dress and a big hat, well, they'd probably assume she was someone's eccentric aunt.

'Who's the lady in the portrait?'

The guests always asked after her, and with a smile one of her new companions would reply, 'That's Miss Henrietta Nelson. She lived here a long time ago. They say the painting is haunted, you know.'

There was always a giggle at that. Henrietta would sense the guests' frissons of alarm but she just smiled at them, and they soon forgot and threw themselves into the occasion. Yes, Yaxley had always been a good place for a party.

When she had first come to live with her cousins, the Leekes of Yaxley, in 1739, it had felt very different. Henrietta was only five. Her parents'

sudden death in a carriage accident had left her an orphan. Her grandmother was not well, so it was her great aunt at Yaxley Hall who offered to take her in. The house was big and strange, and Great Aunt Margaret was very, very old, and always cross and sharp with Henrietta. There were no other children there, just grown-up cousins who came and went. Only Cousin Nicholas, Great Aunt's son, was married, but no child of his had yet lived. It was hard for Henrietta to remember how lonely and unhappy she'd been, back then.

A year after Henrietta came to Yaxley her great aunt died. Henrietta was dressed in her best, most uncomfortable clothes for the funeral. The house filled with relations and people she didn't know. Then they were taken to the church, where a new family vault had been prepared.

The mourners trooped down the steps following the coffin. It was dark and gloomy, the lamps flickering on the damp brick walls. When the shadows closed in, Henrietta had never been so scared. She was sure that cold, dripping fingers would reach out from the shadows and carry her away into the blackness. Sobbing, she clung to her nurse and buried her face in her coat.

When they got back outside, Henrietta said to herself, 'I'm never going in there again, ever, not even when I'm old and dead like Great Aunt.'

Soon after, Cousin Nicholas and his wife came to live at the Hall, and three years later Henrietta got her greatest wish. A baby boy was born. She adored Seymour, playing with him for hours, teaching him to ride when he was big enough and helping him with his lessons. Then, when Henrietta was seventeen, another baby came, Francis, a half-brother for Seymour, and she doted on him too.

Without her noticing, Yaxley had become her home. Seymour and Francis grew up into sociable and energetic young men, but Seymour was a restless soul. At twenty-nine he married briefly then set off on a grand tour of Europe. On his return Henrietta welcomed him with open arms, but he was still restless, moving himself, Henrietta and Francis between Yaxley, a new house at Groton, near Hadleigh, and the family house in London. Henrietta had never entertained much hope of marriage, so, by now in her forties, she enjoyed the life she had – attending assemblies, entertaining, visiting. Secretly, though, she always preferred being at Yaxley.

When he was only forty-three, in 1786, Seymour died during a visit to the London house. Not for him the Yaxley vault – there was a vault, instead, in St Giles, Camden. Grief-stricken, Henrietta watched the mourners making their way to the doorway down into the darkness. She felt all the old terror that had started with Great Aunt Margaret's funeral returning. It'd been the same at Cousin Nicholas's funeral, and that of his wife. She froze, the fear taking hold of her.

'I'll wait for you here,' she whispered to a solicitous Francis. 'You know I can't bear those dark, dank places. Promise me when my time comes you won't put me in a vault.'

Francis inherited Yaxley, and Henrietta remained there with him. At the age of fifty-two Henrietta was lady of the house. She wasn't slowing down, not a bit of it! There were still assemblies to attend, plays at the theatre in Eye, neighbours to visit and entertain, trips to Norwich and London and riding jaunts around the countryside. She basked in being popular and respected.

To cement their place in posterity Francis engaged an artist, William Johnson, to paint their portraits. Henrietta wore her favourite blue and white gown for the sitting. She tied a little dark ribbon round her neck and put on her best white pleated and beribboned hat. In her hand she held some freshly picked roses from the garden. It was hard work sitting still for so long, smiling without looking silly, but she was pleased with the finished painting. She put it up straight away and often admired it as she passed by.

Henrietta died in 1816 from a fall down the short flight of stairs from her room. She was eighty-two. Francis kept his promise: sparing no expense, he arranged for a private mausoleum to be built for her in the grounds of the Hall. The little gothic building was nicely placed beside the path to the church and within sight of the house itself. As her remains were laid inside Henrietta's spirit was grateful. She listened to Francis's sorrowful words in his funeral oration, expressing his devotion to the woman he thought of as aunt and sister, and she wished she could have gone on a little longer. It had never been in her nature to lie around doing nothing. She still wanted to be in the thick of things, to see what was going on. So she spent much of her time haunting her portrait.

When Francis married at long last, Henrietta was so pleased. His daughter was named Henrietta after her. She wasn't forgotten! A smile bloomed across the portrait. It positively beamed.

When the young girl grew up and married, change came to Yaxley. Henrietta mourned the passing of Francis in 1836, disappointed that his spirit didn't join hers in haunting the house. Francis's daughter, young Henrietta, and her husband had plans to live elsewhere. Looking out from her portrait, Henrietta was alarmed to see the furniture being labelled with numbered stickers. They even stuck one on her!

Worse was to come. She sensed her little stone mausoleum invaded. Men tore up the floor, lifted out her coffin. Placing it on a cart, they set off to the church. Henrietta's spirit flew out of the house in a panic and raced after the cart. Where were they taking her?

'They don't want that mausoleum thing there, bor, that be the truth of it,' muttered one of the men, as they hefted the coffin into the church. 'Too gruesome-like for the new owners.'

The door to the vault was open, the way down dark, the smell of damp strong.

The old unreasoning panic assailed her.

'No! No! Not the vault!' she cried.

She felt darkness smother her as they carried her bones down. Her spark of consciousness started to fade … Forcing herself upwards, she shot back to the mausoleum and clung to the walls. But more men came. With sledgehammers they began breaking it down. She raced back into her portrait, her last refuge. The smile was gone, her face cold and angry.

'They will not take me from you,' she promised the portrait. 'Wherever you go, I'll go, even if we have to leave our dear Yaxley.'

When the picture was taken down from the wall it got knocked carelessly against a chair. Henrietta did not see the small flake of paint that fell to the floor, but she felt a jolt and a sudden sense of loss. The flake was gusted away by the wind. Even if Henrietta and her portrait were gone, unbeknown to the spirit in the portrait, a tiny trace of them was left at Yaxley, mindlessly roaming the house and grounds.

The move left Henrietta as lost and confused as the five year old she'd once been. Her portrait sat on the wall of a family friend in Norfolk for many years. She stayed within the painting, afraid to be separated from this one familiar thing. People began to say the sad-faced woman in the portrait was watching them.

One day men with numbered stickers came again. Henrietta was unhooked from the wall and propped up in a tent in the garden with the rest of the household effects. She stared miserably out from her picture as strangers milled about, poking and prodding at the things on display. Then she was held aloft, there was a short volley of words and she was borne away to another house.

She had vowed to stay with her portrait, and that's what she did. Her new custodians kept moving. It was very unsettling; just as she'd resigned herself to a place, they took her off somewhere else. Her spirit took to wandering these new houses. She longed for Yaxley and she felt oddly incomplete, as if a little part of herself was missing. Once, as she gazed out of a window, she saw the owner staring back at her. She became aware of him seeing her as she moved around the house. He didn't seem unduly alarmed. What upset people was her sad face in the portrait. Yet, if someone said something nice about her, she might smile, and that confused them all the more. She didn't care. All she wanted was to go home.

But what was this? The house was being packed up again. Henrietta and her portrait were wrapped, carefully this time, then unwrapped once more in a room with a crowd of people and a man with a hammer.

Where will we be going now? she wondered.

As they wrapped her up again, her spirit rebelled at the constriction of the layers of tissue and bubble wrap, but she didn't dare leave the painting. Footsteps approached and then she heard voices as she was lifted up.

'This one's not going with that shipment to America after all. Private sale, it seems. The buyer was desperate to have it.'

Oh, well, thought Henrietta. Someone must like me!

From inside the wrapping she could feel the motion of a vehicle. When they stopped, she heard doors opening and closing as she was carried somewhere. The wrapping was removed.

All at once she knew. She looked around in wonder, feeling as if a missing part of her had been restored. It was Yaxley Hall. She was home.

They hung her in the hallway where she could see everyone who came and went. She smiled happily at her new companions, two charming young men who reminded her of Seymour and Francis.

I shall watch over them as if I were their aunt, she thought.

Like her cousins, they seemed to like a party. The place rang with happy voices at the weddings they hosted.

Henrietta still looks out from her portrait in Yaxley Hall. There are no longer any weddings, her companions having opted for a quieter life. But visitors still come and admire her as she smiles at them. If she has one sadness, it's that her mausoleum is nothing but a neglected ruin hidden in the undergrowth. She visits it sometimes, swirling around it and thinking of her bones lying in that dark, dank vault.

But they're just bones, she says to herself. They don't matter to me now. But I would like to see my mausoleum restored. It was so lovely, how could it offend anyone? I'll have to have a quiet word with my young men. Another folly in the garden? Why not? Just think of all the parties we could have!

13 The Suffolk Rising

It was growing late, but Becky and Robin loved evening strolls. They'd picked their Icklingham B&B for the easy access on to the heath, and they were studying the map as they made their way along the avenue of willows and oaks at the end of West Street.

'There's a Temple Bridge there,' said Becky. 'I wonder what that means.'

The rest of their walk was spent speculating what the temple might have been. Romano-British? A druidic grove? Or something more recent?

When they reached the Lark, they couldn't see a bridge. In the dusk they could just make out some cracked stone on the other side, where the bridge must once have been. Now, there were just pipes crossing the river. They felt a little cheated.

However, there was a footbridge a little further along. Crossing it, they went on to the heath and watched the sun set, enjoying this special time alone. As they watched, though, they saw, coming across the darkening heath, a horse and rider.

There was something strange about the horseman. At first they thought he was hunched over the horse, but as he drew closer they saw the truth.

Becky clutched at Robin's arm. 'Robin …'

'Yes, I see it too.'

The rider had no head.

And the last rays of the sunset shone right through him.

After they'd legged it back to their room, Becky cried, 'I can't believe what we just saw!' but as she spoke she was she flipping open her tablet, turning on the wi-fi and beginning to search.

Robin went to the window and stared out at the heath, now swathed in darkness.

England exploded into revolt in June 1381. From Essex and Kent the ordinary folk marched on London with bows and arrows, staffs and staves, to demand fairer taxation and wages.

John de Cambridge, Prior of Bury St Edmund's Abbey, was waiting anxiously for news when the breathless young messenger burst into his office.

'My lord, London is afire with rioters!' he cried. 'Worse, that rebel priest John Wrawe is in Long Melford and he's marching on Bury. He and his force were over the border in Essex – sacking and rioting – but now they're in Suffolk. They went to Cavendish, where the traitor priest let them into the church. Your friend, the justice, John of Cavendish, he'd hidden his treasure in the tower, but they've stolen it, and it's said that John Wrawe is wearing my lord of Cavendish's coat worth twenty-five marks! The only reason I'm here before them is that they stopped at Unwin's in Melford Green to drink a pipe of wine!'

When the lad had sought the safety of the abbey, John sank down with his head in his hands. If the rioters were coming to Bury, they would surely come for him. He knew of this Wrawe – another of these heretical priests preaching that all men are equal, inciting the peasants to throw off the yoke of bondage and be free. John's lips pursed in anger. Each man had his place, ordained by God. Had not the Death taught these fools that to question God's law was to bring doom and damnation upon them? Even here in Bury the townsfolk railed against the Church's rightful tithes and taxes.

His heart quailed, thinking of his friend. God willing John was safely away from these madmen. They hated the wealthy. So he had gathered in the poll tax – what of it? It was Parliament's right to collect taxes for the war. Did these fools want the French to overrun the country?

There was no respect for authority these days. The townsfolk viewed the abbey with sullen malice. All that upstart Brounfeld's fault. The prior's thoughts went back to that awful week two years past when Brounfeld had come claiming that the Pope had declared him Abbot of Bury. Arrant nonsense – he, the prior, had declared, as was his right, that Subprior Timworth was abbot! A pang of regret ran through him. If only things hadn't deteriorated so fast! Angry words at the chapter meeting, someone had knocked against someone and the next he knew Brounfeld was out on the streets claiming his brethren had tried to murder him! Into the abbey the townsfolk had poured – Alderman Thomas Halesworth the worst of the lot, always ready to grab advantage for the town. Only the threat of fines kept them out.

The town was a tinderbox – one spark and it would be alight. That spark was John Wrawe.

The prior stared out at the bright afternoon sky. A blackbird was singing in the tree by his window. The strains of choir practice for evensong this Corpus Christi came from the church. For a moment their sweet sounds mingled. It was hard to imagine that his ordered existence could truly change.

At dusk the rebels came.

From the steps of the great abbey gateway the small black-clad figure of John Wrawe shouted out to the crowds: 'Join with us to overthrow this foul corruption we see before us!'

The voice of Thomas Halesworth rose in answer: 'Yes! Let us take what is ours!'

To the monks cowering inside, the walls of their abbey seemed very thin as the roar from the crowds grew louder and darkness fell.

John de Cambridge wasn't there. He'd already fled, abandoning his monks to face the townsfolk's fury.

To the abbey's house at Mildenhall he rode. The servants, wide-eyed with fear at his news, bolted the door behind him.

The next day was a long one. John started at every noise, but Mildenhall lay quiet until late into the afternoon. Then he heard shouts and cheers. In those shouts he heard a name – his own.

'They've come for you, my lord,' said the servant sent out to investigate. He'd returned trembling and white. 'And – your friend, John of Cavendish, he's dead. They have his head on a pole and they're carrying it to Bury. They say they caught him doing his rounds, exhorting more money, near Lakenheath. He fled, they say, but they got him by the river. There was a boat – he ran, but a woman pushed the boat away – and – and that was it for him.'

The prior stared at the servant in horror.

'John's dead?' he whispered. 'They killed him?'

The servant, wide-eyed, said, 'My lord, their blood is up – and it's you they want next.'

When he was gone John stood listening to the shouts and chanting from the town. He could smell smoke now. Were they burning the town?

He had to leave.

His only hope was do what he was sure John had been trying to do – get on to the waterways and make for the Isle of Ely, where the abbey would shelter him in its Fenland fastness.

As darkness fell, a guide was brought to him, a short, dark man, shifty-eyed; a fenlander for sure.

'I'll get you out,' he said, spitting on the ground.

John recoiled, but what choice did he have but to go with him?

As soon as they were out on the street a band of men raced past, whooping and swishing torches at them. Houses were burning; the thick smoke caught in John's throat as his guide slipped them through the streets and down to the wharf.

When they got there, a bank of torches faced them.

'Hand him over!'

John backed away, but his guide grabbed his sleeve, and pushed him behind him. He crouched, heart hammering, as the torches waved above him and men shouted. He heard the clashing of steel against steel. Then he was hauled up. He caught a glimpse of his guide's face, ghastly in the torchlight, and then they were off, the man dragging him tripping and stumbling along behind him. There were men everywhere, torches waving, faces ugly in the torchlight. Blank with terror, John let his guide haul him this way and that.

Another scuffle, and a knife nicked his arm, the pain shocking. For a moment he stood, unbelieving, amid the chaos as the blood soaked into his sleeve. Was it only yesterday he'd heard the choir singing from his study? Then his guide pulled him on again and the nightmare continued.

Eventually they got back to the manor stables. They raced away from the smoke and noise into the quiet of the night. Scarce three miles they'd ridden when the guide stopped them by a wood.

'Let's get in here,' the man murmured. 'We're near Freckenham – far enough away to be safe.'

They led the horses in through the trees, then the guide said, 'You rest yourself, my lord. All my provisions were on that boat, so I'll need to go off and get more. Then to Newmarket we'll go, you mark my words.'

Then he was gone, leaving John alone with his horse in the darkness.

How long he waited he didn't know. It seemed for ever. He jumped at every snapping twig, every rustling branch. All around were the cries of the night creatures. He cowered against his horse in fear.

When he heard the sound of hooves again he jumped up, elated with relief. Then he froze, listening. Surely he was hearing the sound of more than one horse? And – there – what sounded for all the world like the banging of a drum ...

A voice cried out: 'Where lurks the traitor?'

Betrayed! Like a frightened rabbit he ran, darting, heart racing, between the trees. But it was too late. The men surrounded him, and his guide bore down on him, his face full of hate.

'Come along, my lord. There's a reckoning awaiting you.'

They slung him on to a horse, twisted rough ropes around his wrists and waist. Then through the endless night they rode, reaching

Newmarket in the wee small hours before the midsummer dawn. They dragged him to a building and flung him down on filthy straw.

A stinging slap bit his face in the darkness.

'Prophesy who smote you!' came a voice.

All around he heard cruel laughter.

Someone thrust a burning torch in his face and he saw they were kneeling.

'Hail, master!' they cried, amid gales of laughter.

They teased him with water, then splashed it away, constantly shook and slapped him, heedless of his exhaustion.

In the morning they hauled him back on his horse and led him back the way they'd come, to Mildenhall.

'They're all waiting for you there,' hissed his erstwhile guide. 'Then you shall get what's yours – payment for all the wrongs you've done. Bled us dry, you have. Now it's your turn.'

John tried to make his numbed brain form prayers, but the terror and exhaustion were too great.

It was mid-morning before they reached Mildenhall. By the riverside a gang of men were waiting for him.

'Kill the traitor!' they cried.

Among the crowds were Bury men – Thomas of Halesworth was one – with hate in their faces.

With them stood a small man in cleric's clothes, his face drawn with tiredness and his eyes full of zeal. This had to be John Wrawe. The man gave him a look of pity – and at that John felt a shard of ice go through him as his true predicament struck him.

He would die today.

They led him across the heathland, the gorse and broom in full flower, the June sunshine filling the air with the scent of honey. Near the River Lark and the sad remains of the old Knights Templar hall, they stopped.

The trial was a foregone conclusion. As he listened to the litany of accusations of extortion and over-taxation, John felt his soul shrivel inside him. They truly saw him as this bad? All he had wanted was what was best for the abbey.

John Wrawe gazed at him the whole time, that same pity in his eyes throughout, even when Thomas Halesworth spat out the guilty verdict.

A terrified priest had been brought from Icklingham across the river to listen to his sins. The man's voice shook as he gave absolution, and the words gave John a moment of peace.

But no sooner were the words spoken than he was grabbed and forced to his knees.

He barely had time for terror before the swish of the axe.

Then came the pain, and beyond the pain, darkness fell into the morning light.

His body was abandoned there on Cavenham Heath, but his head was carried back to Bury, where it joined the head of his old friend, John of Cavendish. On pikes, the heads were paraded round the town and, for the townsfolk's amusement, made to kiss in friendship and whisper to each other. At last they were set on a pillory and the townsfolk pelted them with refuse.

For eight days the heads stayed there, and for eight days John de Cambridge's body lay on the heath by the Templar Bridge. Although there were birds and dogs aplenty, the body was left alone. Perhaps they sensed the spirit hadn't left.

Throughout that time, chaos reigned in Suffolk, but by the eighth day William de Ufford, Earl of Suffolk, had put down the rising and thrown the ringleaders in gaol. Only then did the abbey's servants creep out from Mildenhall to retrieve their master's body.

John de Cambridge's body was reunited with his head and buried in the peaceful abbey graveyard by the Lark in Bury, but his spirit did not follow. He could not rest. His spirit roams the heath, headless, lost from God's grace, locked in his last days. He's seen at sunset riding his horse towards the bridge, but he never crosses.

Becky closed her tablet with a snap.

'That's a terrible story,' she said, going to Robin as he stood staring out of the window. 'It's hard to imagine, isn't it – everything just erupting like that? All that violence, all that anger …'

Robin folded her into his arms, but he kept on staring out at the dark heath. 'Not really, no,' he said. 'It's all too easy …'

14

The Chiming Hours

Even as a little lad, George Spindler was a helpful boy. He was always busy, tending the chickens, feeding the pig, nursing the runt by the kitchen range. He loved to lend a hand when his father was carting straw to and from the farms. One day, heading home to Westleton along the narrow lanes, Da turned a corner and George saw something coming the other way. It was the hearse, and it filled the road. Top-hatted Mr Boggis was at the reins, whip in hand, the black horses were briskly stepping, the carriage with its plumes and fringes swaying. To George's astonishment, his father was driving straight on.

George grabbed his sleeve and yelled, 'Da, Da, pull in! Thas the hearse a comin'.' His voice rose in panic. 'Da, it won't get past!'

His father laughed. 'What yew a-gooin' on about, lad? There ent no hearse.'

George stared at his da. Why couldn't he see it? The vehicle was upon them. George gritted his teeth for the impact, but it never came. As he opened his eyes the hearse faded away into the sunshine.

His father, never a man of many words, lifted his cap and scratched his head.

'Boy, you're a rum'un all right. A dose of your ma's tonic, thas what yew need.'

George sat pale and silent till they reached home.

'I think the boy's sickening for something,' called his father as they got in, then stomped back out to the yard.

Under his mother's sympathetic gaze the story came out.

'It was so real, Ma,' George said tearfully. 'Then it was gone.'

His mother dusted her floury hands on her apron and looked long and hard at her son.

'You're a big boy now, George. Seven this spring, aren't you? Well, now, I think you're old enough to know.'

She sat down, pulled him close and wiped his tear-stained face.

'The night you were born I had my pains for hours. The midwife, she were a bit worried that you were taking so long to come. Then, just as the church clock was chiming the midnight hour, into the world you came. When the midwife handed you to me she said, "This little mite has been born with the gift of the Chiming Hours. That'll make him kind and hard-working but he'll also be able to see what others can't. They say that those born in the Chiming Hours can see the souls of the departed as they cross over."

'I was alarmed, but she told me it was no curse, but a blessing. You're a kind, hard-working boy, George, but till now I never saw a hint of the other thing. I think you've grown into your gift. It's a special thing, my lad, but others, like your da there, they'll find it strange, so best keep it a secret just for you and me.'

George was not quite sure he understood, but his mother had believed him, and that's what mattered. He vowed that if he should see such things again he'd never breathe a word of them.

In Wenhaston Blackheath, six miles from Westleton, Eliza Goddard needed some help on her smallholding. Her husband had died suddenly, but there was no time to play the weeping widow, not with three young children and the farm to run. It was not in her nature to be sentimental when the practicalities of life had to be dealt with. She wasn't looking to marry again, but the farm was too much to manage alone. She needed a good, trustworthy man. So she asked about, and George Spindler came along to lend a hand.

He was exactly what she'd wanted: a hard-working man, kind to the children and animals. Against her better judgement, they became close and had two children together. She had to admit they complemented each other: no-nonsense Eliza and diligent George. But there was something … odd about him. He'd have funny turns, when he would go all quiet and shivery.

He came home pale and shaken one day after delivering coal to Albion House in Wenhaston.

'Whatever is wrong, George?' Eliza cried.

'Vicar were there,' he muttered.

'Has someone died?'

'No, it were a laying.'

It was like getting blood from a stone! Look at him shuffling away as if he had some guilty secret!

'What sort of laying? You mean a laying out?'

She saw his face harden for a moment. 'No, laying a ghost.'

Eliza caught hold of his arm, pulled him back. 'Oh, George, you don't believe that old nonsense, do you?'

'It had a top hat and whip, it did, 'Liza, a top hat and whip.'

With those baffling words he marched out to see to the horse.

'I don't know what to make of you, George Spindler,' Eliza said to the empty air. 'I truly don't.'

They never married. Eliza liked to say that a fortune-teller had twice warned her against it. She was her own woman now, and no man was going to take away her independence … and there was that feyness about George that gave her pause.

Married or not, they lived well and Eliza's fields flourished. They had more than they needed to feed their growing family. Eliza was quick to spot an outlet for her surplus flour. In Wenhaston at that time many men worked on the land in high season, then went to the fishing during the winter. The wives left at home often struggled to put food on the table while they waited for the pay packets to come. Eliza started selling to these less fortunate women, but she remembered her own thin days. If they could not pay, their names and what they owed were chalked on a board in the barn, to pay when they could.

However, flour began to go missing in the night and names on the board had been rubbed out without payment being made. She wasn't going to stand for that! So she took a broom and an old sheet, and fashioned a ghost-like scarecrow. She set it up in the barn where the draught from the door would catch the cloth. It looked pretty convincing in the half-light.

'That'll larn 'em,' she chuckled.

That very evening she heard someone at the barn door. She quickly put out her light and slipped into the shadows beside the barn. The door was slowly pushed open and a cloaked figure with a dim lantern crept inside. As they did so the light fell on the sheet rippling around the broomstick and there was a strangled cry as the woman dropped the bag she was carrying, ran out the door and was off down the lane. Eliza returned to the house highly satisfied. Once or twice more she found the door ajar and bags of flour dropped on the floor, but then the stealing stopped.

'Don't go up the lane from Well Green to the heath at dusk,' she heard neighbours saying. 'There's ghosts!'

Eliza's older children were always a bit lazy. Young Fred could've happily idled his life away, but George's gentle chivvying wouldn't let him. The lad was good with his hands, always whittling away at a piece of wood, so George had a word with a local carpenter and a job was secured. His mother was pleased, and Fred enjoyed the work, but he and his mates still liked a drink after work. They patronised both the Star in Blackheath and the Compasses in Wenhaston.

One evening, well oiled, they left the Compasses and set off on their usual shortcut across the churchyard to the heath. They'd only got as far as the darkness of the yews when from among the gravestones came the most awful moaning and groaning, like a soul in torment. Fred and his chums stopped dead in their tracks. The long shadows of the church and the trees came and went as clouds scudded across the moon. They could see no one, but the eldritch moaning continued, as if drawn from the bowels of the earth.

'What's that?' hissed Peter Canham.

'Dunno,' Jack Kemp whispered back, 'but I ent gooin' no further.'

'Me neither,' said Fred. The three turned back to the road and ran full pelt down Star Hill.

The next night, as they cooled their heels in the Star, Fred, Peter and Jack saw people looking at them and laughing. Turned out it'd been that Tommy Aldous that lodged up at Church Farm. He'd fallen into a newly dug grave and was moaning and groaning away while they were cowering. He'd heard everything they'd said, and now the story was about that they thought there was a Wenhaston ghost.

'That Tommy, just wait till he comes down to the Star,' said Fred. 'We'll give him some of his own medicine!'

Fred well remembered his mother's scarecrow ghost that had seen off the flour thieves. He and his sibs had swiped it one night to do some scaring on Well Lane, and had given old Tilley such a fright. So he found some sheets and, while Tommy was safely quaffing his ale in the Star, Fred and his chums got themselves draped up and waited for their victim to head home across the heath. When they loomed up out of the night around him poor Tommy ran for his life.

They heard at the Compasses that Tommy'd sworn never to drink at the Star again.

The next time he was at his mother's house, Fred was entertaining the family with these adventures when George came in. His face was ghastly, and he was shivering. The laughter died away.

'I've just seen Mrs Girling down Hog Lane,' he told them. 'She looked real bad, sort of funny about the eyes.'

'What, just now? But you can't have done,' said Fred. 'She died last night. I was at her laying out to measure for the coffin this morning.'

Eliza took in George's ashen face and trembling hands and remembered how he'd been the same when they'd had that strange conversation about the ghost laying. She'd never had much truck with talk of ghosts. But this sounded real. It was unsettling and Eliza didn't like being unsettled.

George's thoughts were still full of Mrs Girling. When the familiar dizzy feeling had come, when she'd not returned his greeting, he'd guessed she'd gone. Now Fred's words had proved it. He sighed. It might be unsettling, but it was his gift, the secret he'd hidden all his life, even from his lover – the gift of the Chiming Hours.

15

The Ghosts of Landguard Fort

Theodore 'Teddy' Beard had always been a light-fingered cove, fingers always dipping into places they shouldn't go and pulling out things that weren't his. Dad had done a runner when Teddy was only six. He and Mum had to shift for themselves after that. She'd found it hard to put food on the table and pay the rent at the same time, so that's when Teddy started to help with a little bit of this and a little bit of that.

In 1914 Teddy turned seventeen, and when war broke out he joined up as soon as he could wangle it. The army promised him a shiny new uniform and, more importantly, three square meals a day! But he wasn't stupid. A Bedford lad, he joined the 3rd Bedfordshires knowing full well that they were on coastal defence. Instead of going to France, he was sent to Felixstowe.

Landguard Fort was an imposing place, proper historic, its solid bulk sitting hard on the edge of Suffolk, looking out at the port of Harwich across the point where the rivers Stour and Orwell meet. Over there in Harwich the navy had their ships.

Teddy and his mates spent their time constructing earthworks and trenches, creating entanglements of barbed wire and building redoubts and pillboxes. The Boche wasn't going to take Harwich, no chance! Teddy revelled in the work, enjoying the physicality of it, and the camaraderie of his new mates. He made a vow that there'd be no more thieving, cos it wasn't right to thieve from your mates, and, besides, a man'd have to be suicidal to thieve in his own barracks.

Marching through the fort's tunnel-like entrance made Teddy feel like a real soldier. Inside, though, something about the place made him uneasy. The high walls and the long, ill-lit tunnels seemed to close in on him. He was grateful that he and the lads were bivouacked out in the barracks below the fort. But as the months went by and more and more wounded were brought to the fort, Teddy and his mates were moved inside, packed in the fort like sardines in a tin. Teddy didn't like it, but he had to lump it.

One night, when he was patrolling on the Holland Bastion, enjoying the air and the moonlit sea, he sensed that he was no longer alone. Thinking it a messenger, he span about to attention – and nearly fell over his own feet in surprise. For there, standing beside the battlement just where Teddy had been a moment before, was a man. He was surely not of his regiment, since he wore a long yellow coat slung with a bandolier, a wide-brimmed hat and red leggings, and he was pointing a strange-looking gun out to sea. It was hard to see well in the moonlight, but as Teddy stared he realised he could see the brickwork through the man, and a gasp escaped his lips.

The man vanished.

How Teddy got through the rest of his shift he didn't know. As soon as his relief came he raced to the mess room. There, taking his ease, sat a sergeant he'd not met before. Dark-haired, about ten years older than Teddy, with old-fashioned sideburns and 'tache, he was sitting in his shirt and braces.

'What's up, lad?' said the sergeant. 'You look like you've seen a ghost!'

Teddy went white. How did the man know?

'Blimey, you 'ave, 'aven't you?'

Teddy gave a sheepish little nod, fully expecting a ribbing.

'You were up on 'olland Bastion, weren't you? Well, you've 'ad a baptism tonight, lad. Everyone sees 'im, faithful old soldier that 'e is. Want to know 'ow long 'e's bin up there? Two hundred and fifty years!'

The sergeant gestured to a pot and mug on the table. Hesitantly, Teddy poured himself what turned out to be a thin cocoa and sank down on a stool.

'It was when we were at war with the Dutch – 1667, it was, last time an invading army set foot on our shores – and please God, let it be the last! Eight hundred troops they landed, and only two hundred of our boys at the fort, but we 'eld 'em off, we did, and only one of ours, a musketeer, died. That's 'im up there, still guarding after all these years. I don't reckon 'e knows 'e's dead.'

After that it seemed to Teddy that once he'd 'tuned in' he couldn't tune out.

Walking across the bridge to the fort one time, he'd had to flatten himself against the rail as a coach and horses, all plumes and livery, rattled at top speed over the bridge. When he'd got inside, there was no sign of it. Another time, he'd seen a white horse galloping over the scrubby dunes by the rifle ranges below the fort. He'd raised the alarm, as the poor thing might get accidently shot. But there was no trace of it – not even hoof prints.

Then there was Chapel Bastion. Down the bottom of it were store-rooms: dark, windowless, bowels-of-the-earth kind of places. Three rooms running off each other, each darker than the next. Teddy hated them, but you had to obey if you were ordered to fetch something.

Going into the second room, he set his lantern on a shelf and began to search through the boxes to find what was needed. As he searched, he became aware of a whimpering. Grabbing the lantern, he wheeled about.

'Who's there? You all right?'

There was no one. He checked the third room, but there was nothing. Setting his lantern back on the shelf, he resumed his search, but the sound came back. As he listened, he realised it was sobbing, not whimpering. Constant, hopeless sobbing. He realised with a sinking feeling, that this was another of his 'turns'. As if conjured by the thought, a voice issued out of the darkness.

'Mother, I asked them, I swear I did, I told them to tell you … O mother, why won't you come?'

He swung the lantern up again. There in the corner, for a flick of time, he saw it. A crouching figure in a tattered and stained nightshirt, shoulders heaving with sobs.

He grabbed the lantern and fled. Orders be damned!

His feet took him back up to the mess room. Sitting there again, in his braces and shirt and those odd high-waisted trousers, was the sergeant.

'O sarge!' gasped Teddy. 'O sarge!'

The sergeant gestured up at a bottle on a shelf. With trembling hands Teddy poured himself a tot of brandy and sank down in a chair to tell his tale.

'Ah, the plague boy,' said the sergeant when he'd done. 'They locked 'im up there, they did, fag end of the eighteenth century when we was out discovering all sorts o' new places, and new diseases to boot. That lad came back from foreign parts all fevered and spotty. They 'ad no idea what was wrong so they locked 'im up in the bastion to get well – or die. They say 'e begged for 'is mum to be told, but they wouldn't do it, cos they feared there'd be a panic. So 'e died there all alone, poor beggar.'

After that, Teddy found it more and more difficult to keep to his mended ways. Never mind the war, his nerves were shot by the ghosts! His light fingers started to get into pockets and under pillows to find illicit packets of fags and bars of chocolate. Soon enough he was thieving handkerchiefs and wallets. Each time he vowed never again, but he just couldn't stop himself.

One night when he was patrolling on top of Chapel Bastion, just in the act of blowing his nose on a stolen hanky, he felt a rush of air beside him. He whirled around to see a woman rush past. She ran to the battlements and, before he could move, flung herself over. He raced there and stared down. But there was nothing to be seen in the dry moat below, and he realised she'd been dressed in big skirts and with her hair all piled up. Besides, there were no women at the fort, worse luck.

He didn't rush straight to the mess room this time. He just brooded on it alone in bed at night. Not a sound she'd made as she'd fallen.

Two nights later, he saw it again – the woman racing past, flinging herself over ... The next day, when he was sent back into the bastion's storerooms, and he was all braced for the plague boy, who should he see but the woman, pacing back and forth and muttering to herself in some foreign lingo.

Back to the mess room he went. There was the sergeant. Odd how he'd never seen him anywhere else. It was as if the fellow lived in there!

'You're a right one, aren't you?' said the sergeant after Teddy had explained what he'd seen. 'This was all back in the eighteenth century when Sir Philip Thicknesse was the guv'nor – and 'e was worse, 'e was, than even your usual type o' guv'nor, always off in London and Bath, currying favour and not doing 'is job. Well, there was women in the fort in those days, wives and the like, and one o' them 'ad this fancy lace 'anky, and she was always flashing it about. Course, it went missing. The chief suspect was the paymaster sergeant's wife. Portuguese, she was, Catholic, o' course, and couldn't speak the lingo that well. The rest o' the women hated 'er. She said she was innocent, and 'er husband backed 'er up, but no one believed them. So, 'e tried to take matters into 'is own 'ands, and 'e left the fort to get 'elp – without asking permission, and you know what that means, doncha?'

'Court martial,' whispered Teddy.

'Aye, and they say he went up against the wall like a man, but after 'e'd bin shot, it sent 'er off 'er 'ead, it did, and she flung 'erself off the Chapel Bastion.'

It wasn't until he came away that it struck Teddy. A stolen handkerchief? He'd been blowing his nose on a stolen hanky himself. It was a warning! He vowed never to steal again.

Then the news came. The worst news. The 3rd Beds' time as coastal defence was up. They were going to France.

Teddy was terrified. Hadn't he seen the wounded coming back? And they were the lucky ones! Something snapped inside him. One night he found himself with someone's pocket watch in his hand. This time he was seen, and by men who were as on edge as he was.

Next morning, as he washed his face in the washroom by Chapel Bastion, the light from the doorway was blotted out and he looked up to see three big, strapping lads from his bunkroom.

'You dirty little thief,' cried the owner of the watch. 'Think you can steal from me? Well, think again. We've come to teach you a lesson.'

Teddy cringed away from the fist coming at him, but there was nothing he could do.

He awoke to find himself in the bath next door. The beating was sharp in his mind, but as he eased himself out of the tub he didn't hurt at all. He felt strange, though. It wasn't something he could put his finger on; just ... strange.

It was very quiet, too. Usually there was always some noise about the fort, even late at night, but all he could hear was the shushing of the sea, even though the light seemed very bright. He closed his eyes to try and drive away the strangeness.

When he opened them he was no longer alone.

In front of him was a group of people. His heart chilled. He recognised them.

There was the musketeer in his yellow coat. There the young lad in his stained nightshirt, his face all pocked. There the woman with her dark hair piled up and her full skirts. And, O Christ, there was the sergeant, in his braces and shirt. As if for the first time, Teddy took in the old-fashioned cut of his trousers, his fancy moustache and sideburns. He looked like a sergeant out of his grandma's picture books. Why had he never noticed it before? As he realised that the sergeant wasn't what he'd seemed, he realised something else as well. He knew, he just knew, what had happened to him.

He wouldn't be going to war.

But he would never leave the fort.

Sarge's eyes were full of compassion as he held out a hand and beckoned.

'Welcome Teddy,' he said. 'Come and join us.'

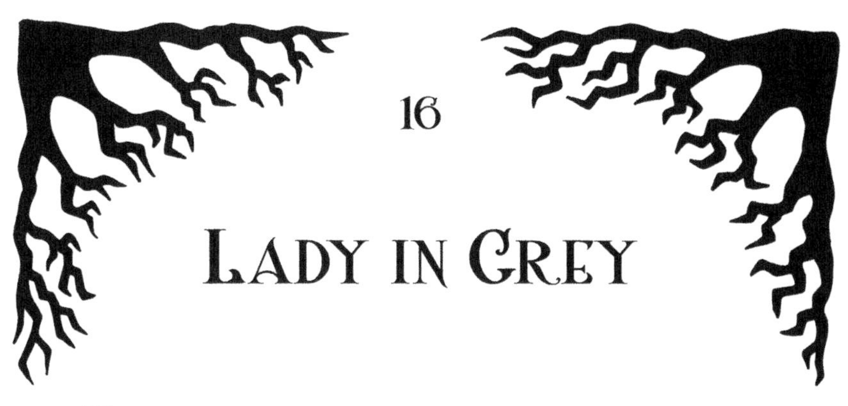

16

Lady in Grey

I'm tired now, very tired, and I don't walk much these days, but I do remember. I'm still here in my home. I've never known anything else, though once I longed for change.

Blythburgh Lodge was a lonely place in which to grow up. I loved my home, but it was isolated, in neither Walberswick nor Blythburgh, farmland on one side and the Westwood Marshes on the other. My brothers had it easier, off doing the things that young men could do. I didn't even have the company of other girls, save the maids, whom I watched with envy as they laughed and chattered on their way home to their villages.

I was allowed to ride, though. I loved the excitement it gave me, my one freedom. Back at the stables, Sam, the stablehand, would help me down from the saddle and make sure my horse was groomed. He wasn't like the maids. We were much of an age and he didn't know to behave differently with me. He was always friendly and smiling. He was my only friend, and I, I believe, was his.

When we were about sixteen, everything changed. I don't know what caused it. His hand on my waist, perhaps, helping me into the saddle. A lingering glance as I left. Suddenly what we had went far beyond friendship. We were caught in a passion for each other and would take every chance we could to meet. We knew the danger, or thought we did. We didn't care. We thought we were clever enough to foil them all.

But my brothers soon realised what was going on. William, my eldest brother, spoke to me in his grave way, warning me it must stop. If it didn't, my father would have to know. William was fifteen years older than me and understood nothing of what I felt. My body and soul yearned for Sam and Sam alone.

I paid William no mind. Sam was waiting for me at the Old Covert. All I could think of were his strong arms around me, his lips on mine. My brother followed me, cruelly waiting until I was in Sam's arms before he wrenched me away and marched me straight to my father.

The disappointment in my father's eyes cut me to the bone, but for Sam's sake I made myself raise my chin. We'd been found together – if I was disgraced, then I would have to marry Sam, wouldn't I?

His next words crushed my hope.

'Samuel will be dismissed immediately. He'll not work in the county again. You are to be confined to the house until he is gone.'

Sam dismissed! Barred from working! What would happen to him? I tried to protest but Father would not allow me to speak.

'You will be going to your Aunt Martha in Ipswich until a suitable husband is found for you. God willing we will be able to keep this scandal to ourselves.'

I remember the clock striking midday as I ran from the room to the refuge of my bedchamber on the top floor. My window had a view of the stables. I could see Sam struggling and hear his angry words as they pushed him out on to the road. He turned to look at the house, but the sun was on the window, and I knew he wouldn't be able to see me. His face was desolate, the twin of mine own.

The little window that had opened in my life was now firmly closed. Aunt Martha was a strict, God-fearing woman. She already thought me flighty, I knew. Her house would be a prison, my disgrace her pleasure. And after that? Marriage against my will. All I wanted was for everything to go back to how it was, but it was hopeless. A void of emptiness opened up before me.

My eyes strayed to my Bible. Perhaps God would give me guidance. The book fell open at Job, chapter 7: 'Is there not an appointed time to man upon earth?' A shiver ran down my spine. The chapter went on to speak about days without hope.

'The eye of him that hath seen me shall see me no more,' I whispered, my heart thumping in my breast, as if it knew before my mind what I must do.

That night I dressed in my favourite grey silk gown, took a shawl and my Bible. I stole down the stairs and crept into the study, where

I knew the window never closed properly, and slipped outside. In the courtyard everything was shadowy but the surface of the pond in the centre glinted in the pale moonlight. I found a pile of cobbles in a corner, filled my shawl and tied it around my waist. I laid the Bible down open at my chosen text, clearly marked with ink: 'Am I a sea, or a whale, that thou settest a watch over me?'

I stepped into the pond, whispering the last verse of the chapter: 'Thou shall seek me in the morning, but I shall not be.'

I found the cold water strangely soothing. It reached my shoulders, but I did not waver. There was no reason for me to live, not without my Sam. I went down, down, down.

Dimly I became aware of sounds above me. They were searching for me. I was hardly aware of what I was. Time passed, the shouts went on and I wondered why they were searching. I was here. And yet, I felt curiously listless or, rather, detached, as if I wasn't really there. Now I could see the house, the running figures. What puzzled me most was why I was wearing my best grey silk in the middle of the day. And why could they not see me when I was right there?

Then they found the Bible. I saw my brother mouth the verse, saw his face blanch. I saw them bringing the body out.

My body, the stones still in the shawl around my waist.

My brothers and my father gathered round me in silence, then my father cried out, 'My child, my poor child, I drove you to this!'

I ran forward, suddenly full of remorse. But no one saw me and my arms passed right through him. I saw the truth as I looked down at my dead flesh. There would be no marriage against my will. There would be nothing now but this long loneliness.

I could only watch as my family changed over the years. My father died, my brothers married and eventually my family left Blythburgh Lodge. But I remained, tied to the place by invisible threads. I wandered the house and grounds unseen by all who lived there. Sometimes they would shiver as I passed and lamps would flicker, but, after all, an old house is draughty. Tenants came and went. One family, the Browns, had a clock that chimed like my father's. When it struck midday, I'd remember the sound of the clock striking outside my father's study the day that sealed my fate, and I would run to my room just as I had done then. At times like that I was incautious. Mrs Brown said she'd heard me.

Years later came those girls. Lucy and Mabel. I remember all the young daughters of the house, but these girls reminded me more of myself. A new century had just begun, the 1900s. How could so much time have passed and I still be the same? Lucy lived here; Mabel, her cousin, would often come to stay, and they would talk about these bright new futures girls were now allowed. They must have been about twelve years old and shared the bedroom that had once been mine.

'Oh, girls,' I whispered, 'I hope your dreams come true.'

But why should they have what I could never have? Their whole lives were ahead of them, but mine was gone.

One night, while they slept, my jealousy got the better of me. I picked up their neatly folded clothes and in a rage tossed them round the room.

I watched their shocked faces the next morning. Smiled to myself as they blamed each other.

'Ooh, do you think it's the ghost?' wondered Lucy.

'A ghost?' said Mabel. 'That's scary. I don't want to know.'

'Oh, she's not that bad. She's a lady in a grey dress. She never hurts anyone. I think she just wants to play.'

I had to smile at that, my jealousy fading away. But 'a lady in a grey dress'? I must be getting careless!

For a while the house was empty. It was easier in a way, but I missed the people. There were visitors, though. Young men and girls would arrive, a crowd of them, on noisy two-wheeled contraptions – I've never got used to all these new-fangled carriages. With their long hair and bright clothing I found it hard to tell boys from girls! These girls had more freedom than even Lucy and Mabel could have imagined. They ate their food out of paper, drank from bottles and played loud music. They sat around smoking those paper tubes of tobacco – though these ones smelt a bit different. They passed them from one to another, then they would go into a sort of trance. I'd float among them then, not caring if I was seen.

The local constabulary chased them off from time to time.

'You're trespassing – and don't you know this place is haunted?' the officers would call after them.

One night three of those policemen came back on their own. They went all over the house with their bright torches, fixing tape across doorways. Then they settled down in the hallway with candles burning.

'Come on, ghost lady, let's be seeing you!' one of them called out.

I enjoyed myself that night. I blew a cold breeze on them, setting them all a-shiver. Then I moved an old box in an upstairs room to make a noise over their heads. I unhooked the tape from the doorways and stood at the top of the stairs looking down at them. But I didn't let them see me, oh no, and they went away with nothing but a feeling that someone might have been there.

Not long after that my house was rescued from its long abandonment when a new family moved in. They have worked hard to make Westwood Lodge, as it is now known, fine and proud again. I'm still here, but as I said, I'm tired these days and I don't walk much. Maybe it's time for me to go on, but I don't know how. Sometimes I still like to stand by the pond on a pale moonlit night and remember.

17

Monks of the Buttermarket

It was a bright spring day in Ipswich in 1989. Jim and Frank were standing on the corner of The Walk off the Buttermarket and staring through the temporarily open hoarding into the bare open space beyond.

'Well, that's that,' said Jim. 'Forty years' work down the drain.'

'And more than a hundred and fifty years of printing in Ipswich,' grumbled Frank, taking a drag on his cigarette.

'And for what? A shopping centre! I've told the wife she's not to use it. I says to her, "Ethel, you worked there yourself until we was married, and it's paid the bills ever since. Would you really shop there?" But you know how she gets that look ...'

Frank laughed. 'I do that, Jim. But I say good luck to them. It's a sad old day to see Cowells gone, but they might find there's more to the place than meets the eye. Remember that night? More'n thirty years ago. We were working late, weren't we? Just us and the nightwatchman left in the building, and we saw that ... thing.'

There was no humour in Jim's grin. 'I'll not forget that till my dying day! The sight of that white figure drifting towards us in the basement, its robes flapping in some breeze that you and I couldn't feel, the hunted look on its face ... Still gives me the shivers just thinking on it.'

Frank sucked on his cigarette again. 'It came so close I could see the whites of its eyes – and I could see right through it as well! Then – poof! It vanished into thin air. I was all for jacking it in that night – and it was a long time before I'd work into the night again.'

They both stopped as they became aware that a couple of workmen across the street by the entrance to the building site were staring at them. Frank winked at Jim and raised his tweed cap to the men. One of them turned away, but the other walked over to them.

'You used to work here?'

'For our sins,' said Jim. 'We were compositors. Started on the same day, worked there all our working lives. We were lucky – Frank and me were sixty-five last year, so we got out with our pensions intact. It's the young ones I feel sorry for. There's no future in fine printing, these days ...' He stopped, aware that the workman's eyes had glazed over.

After a moment, the man spoke, his Adam's apple bobbing: 'You were saying you saw something ... odd in there?'

Jim and Frank looked at each other, then laughed.

'There was plenty of "odd",' said Jim. 'That old monk was everywhere! The women used to see him, too, when they was packing in the basement. My Ethel used to say he seemed as surprised to see them as they were to see him. She said too that even if he were surprised he got a look in his eye that made her think he liked the look of 'em! But he always disappeared when they screamed ... so they always screamed.'

The workman went pale.

'But – a monk in a printing works?'

'Yes,' said Frank, a gleam in his eye. 'Where you're all digging away, that's the old Whitefriars, the Carmelite friary. It was here on the Buttermarket from the 1200s till old Cromwell shut 'em down in 1538. Why'd you ask?'

The workman shifted uneasily. 'We found bones. Human bones. And, well, I saw something one night. We were working late, had to get that level cleared, and, drifting over the bare earth was this ... figure, in white robes, like you said – like a monk. His face – I swear, I've never seen a face look so, so ...'

'Worried?' supplied Jim.

'That's it.' The workman looked relieved. 'It was just me that saw him, so I thought ...'

'If you found bones, we know about them,' Frank went on. 'Everyone does! Them archaeologists, they'd already been over the place afore Cowells was built. There's important bones down there, old ones, old as that King Raedwald over at Sutton Hoo, and others too. Once, years back, they were doing a bit o' building work, and they found this chamber all sealed off with a load of old bones in it! Gave us all who'd seen the monk a turn, I can tell you, and we were gossiping about some huge massacre of monks back in Henry VIII's day, but the archaeologists said, no, it was just that someone had moved the bones from the monks' cemetery, probably when their church was taken down. Place like this, centre of a town for a thousand years, you've got to expect a few bones! They took the bones away, but the monk he kept coming back.'

The workman didn't look convinced. 'We – we found an old well, too. It was there I saw the monk. But that's just been filled in! The archaeologists didn't even get a chance to look!'

'Oh well,' said Jim. 'I reckon that monk'll be haunting your shopping centre! But I don't think he means any harm. He's just worried. I wish I knew why.'

Subprior William was worried. He'd always been a worrier, but these were worrying times. In other times they'd have elected a new prior after Prior John, old Bilious Bale, left – and they'd have excommunicated the man for his blasphemous embracing of this Protestant faith, and making that woman, Dorothy, his wife! But, no, he'd been given a living at Thorndon in Norfolk, and they, his erstwhile charges, were just expected to muddle along. This year of Our Lord 1537 was already shaping up to be the worst yet. The king was befuddled by that whore Anne Boleyn whispering to him in his bed, telling him to destroy God's work – the monasteries. William kept these thoughts to himself, of course, but he knew everyone was worried. Rich men were queuing up to line their pockets with monastic riches, or so it was whispered among the monks and friars of Ipswich.

As he did each day, he turned the key in the well-oiled lock of the treasure chest, just to assure himself the treasure was still there. But it was diminishing … He'd heard tales, too, of the visitations from the King's Commissioners, how they'd go away with their arms full of deeds and gold.

It was true that the friary was now too big for them, stretching as it did along the Butter Market from St Stephen's Lane to Queen Street. Most of it was empty and crumbling. How he wished he'd known it a hundred years ago! Now no one sent their young men here to learn. What was the point of all the friars' learning if there was no one left to carry it on? Coin by coin their money was disappearing on food and firewood. Soon they'd have to start selling the books.

If they lasted that long.

The friars could see the way the wind was blowing. As they were scholars, some had left to take up teaching positions in the universities. A core clung to the hope that they might stay in their home in Ipswich, but, as they watched their subprior become more bowed with worry, it grew harder and harder to believe that all would be well.

Then one day, Subprior William seemed to change. Suddenly he was upright and smiling. The other friars were alarmed. Had his worrying caused him to lose his wits?

When an application for funds for their daily food was refused, the cellarer decided to check for himself. He crept into the subprior's office, unhooked the key, opened the chest …

Down to his fellow friars he rushed.

'The treasury!' he gasped. 'It's empty! Just a few bags of coppers. There's not enough money to feed the rats, let alone us.'

When the friars challenged the subprior, he just gave them a seraphic smile. 'Were we not a mendicant order at the beginning, brothers? Let us go out and beg for our supper.'

He explained how the friary's funds had been gradually getting worse, but he hadn't wanted to worry them. The friars were aghast. They checked the deeds and documents. A little money was still coming in from the houses they held in the town, but belts had to be severely tightened.

Then the royal visitor came. Dr Ingworth stalked around the friary, his nose in the air as he took in the carved pillars and the broken glazing in the upper walkways. All the paperwork had to be laid before him. When he had finished he gathered all the friars together.

'Such a small body of men needs little. Four pounds per annum is all you need. The Crown needs the money more. I shall be taking these rents.' He gestured at the papers. He was taking more than twenty-eight pounds from them each year in rents.

The friars' poverty increased. They sold the books. By now the only men left were those with no other place to go, and they were going hungry. Poor Subprior William's mind was wandering. The friars watched him pacing the church and muttering about the treasure.

They wrote a letter to Thomas Cromwell, the king's chief minister, begging his assistance. Surely he would understand?

The order of dissolution came in 1538. The friars were told they would all receive a pension, but it was a pittance. Out there in the world they would not have the support of each other – and who would look after the subprior, who was now so sick?

The cellarer was the one who broke the news to the old man. He hardly seemed to take it in. But when the cellarer spoke wistfully of how their treasure chest had once been full, the old man sat bolt upright and an expression of intense worry appeared in his face. It took a long time to quiet him. When the cellarer went down to his brothers he was worried himself.

'It's like he knows something, but, God ease his soul, he can't speak now. You don't think ...' the cellarer paused. 'You don't think he *hid* the money, do you?'

In a fever of excitement they searched the place from top to bottom, but there was no sign.

The next day, when the friars arose for prayer they found the subprior slumped at the bottom of the stairs to the kitchen, a look of deep agitation on his face.

The friars looked at each other in horror. Had he got up to seek the treasure, and fallen in the effort?

Now they'd never know.

It was the end for the Carmelites in Ipswich, the end of the monasteries in England. The friars dispersed, found new lives elsewhere. The friary was rebuilt and reworked many times. Over the centuries, people reported a ghostly presence – a robed figure with a worried expression, who seemed to be searching for something.

The Buttermarket Shopping Centre opened in 1992. The shoppers flocked in, filling the place with talk and bustle. At the end of the day it was Emma Bradbrook's job to go and empty the pay machine in the underground car park. It wasn't a task she particularly enjoyed. The building was all new, the lights all working, but there was something about being down there on your own. It was all too easy to imagine that some man might stay down there, in wait, to go after the money … or worse. But there was CCTV watching.

As always, she chided herself for being silly and got on with unlocking the machine. As she did, she glimpsed something from the corner of her eye. Had that shadow flickered? She turned, but there was nothing. She continued hauling out the money and pouring it into the bag. There it was again, a flicker of movement.

She turned, and the money bag dropped from her hands.

In front of her was the figure of a man. He was staring straight at her. It took a moment to register what she was seeing. A man, yes, but dressed in long robes – like a monk. It was his face that stayed with her. So worried. And, as she stared, she realised she could see right through him …

She screamed.

He vanished.

With as much presence of mind as she could muster she grabbed the money bag and fled upstairs. When she got to the control room, she realised how stupid it sounded to say she'd seen a ghost, so she just talked about the shadows and her worries about theft.

After that, the management always made sure that two people went down to collect the money. But, although no one spoke about it, the night-time CCTV picked up shadows down there where nobody could have been.

18 The Murderess's Daughter

Oulton High House thumped to the sound of disco beats that night until after one in the morning. After a long, hard couple of days at the conference, the delegates were glad to let their hair down and strut their stuff. By half past one they'd all gone. The two DJs, Del and Tony, were left to pack up. They loaded the van as quietly as they could. There'd been complaints about the Saturday night discos, and Del and Tony were keen the management didn't hear any bad reports about tonight.

Tony was already in the van when Del turned off the last light and locked up. He gave his partner a wan smile, started up the van and began backing down the drive.

Tony tensed beside him and cried out, 'Watch out! I can see a woman in the mirror!'

Del braked hard. He peered back. Sure enough, right behind them on the drive stood a woman, blocking the way out. For a second, he thought it must be one of the delegates, and was just about to lean out and ask her to get out of the way when his brain caught up with what his eyes saw.

This was no shoulder-padded, mini-skirted conference delegate. She wore a long, stiff dress as if she'd been to a fancy dress party, but Del was sure she hadn't. The woman was glowing with a bright white light. He stared, unable to believe what he was seeing. But it was true. This woman was floating a foot off the ground.

Del executed the smartest three-point turn of his life. When he swung the van around, she was still there, in front of them now, caught in the headlights, staring straight at them. Del felt a sudden sadness well up in him.

There was only one way out. Straight through what he now had to admit must be a ghost. Del tried to ease round her, but wherever he went the figure was always in front of the van, staring blankly at them. Tony kept up a steady litany of curses beside him.

Suddenly, the thing shot towards them. The windscreen glowed white and they glimpsed a young, tear-streaked face, its mouth open in a scream. A rush of cold passed over them, they both shouted …

Then there was just the quiet and the steady glow of the headlights.

For a long moment the two of them just sat there.

Then Del saw what they'd done. There were tyre tracks all over the lawn, and they were stationed right in the middle of it! Some distant part of his brain registered that there would be trouble for this, but right now he didn't care. He put the van in gear, pressed his foot on the accelerator and drove back to Lowestoft as fast as he could.

It was a very big house for just one young woman, but it was the only home Sophie knew. Once, she'd lived here with her mother and father. She must have been about ten when they'd gone. No matter how hard she tried, she simply couldn't remember what had happened.

Except … she still got nightmares. They were a confusion of shouting and screaming and running feet, but when she woke up she never remembered the dream. She'd asked the servants, but as soon as she began their faces just shut down. Even old Hannah, the housekeeper, who had all but raised her, would say nothing.

Sometimes Sophie would hear noises outside. A hunting horn would sound and she'd hear hounds baying and the pounding of horses' hooves. Running to the window, she'd gaze across the fields to the wooded hills. There were never any huntsmen. Besides, what hunt would take place in the middle of the night? She always thought of her father when she heard the horn. He'd loved to hunt, and she could see him in her mind's eye, his cheeks flushed and rosy from the port he'd supped before setting out.

Sometimes, when she was growing up, she'd really hated the house, but so long as the rent was paid she had to stay. It puzzled her. She wrote to Mr Heythuysen, the landlord, but though he assured her the rent continued to be paid he wouldn't say who was paying it. Now that didn't matter. She would be leaving soon. She would be Martin's bride before the year was out. Hannah lamented that she'd not experienced the society that a squire's daughter should, but Martin's farm was large and prosperous and he himself a good, kind man. It was enough.

That evening Martin dined with her. They'd not yet started the meal when, outside the hall, came a sudden bang. Sophie shot up. She hated loud noises. Then the door to the hall burst open, the fire leapt in the hearth, and there in the doorway was a woman.

Sophie gasped and darkness clouded her vision. Coming to, she realised Martin's hands were holding her up.

The woman was her mother.

She advanced, a sickly-sweet smile on her face.

'My darling little Sophie, how you've grown!'

Sophie stared at her.

'I am *so* sorry I had to leave you alone for so long, my darling,' the woman went on. 'But that doesn't matter now. I've come to take you away.'

'Wha– What?' stammered Sophie. 'Take me away? But – I'm to be married.'

With a brittle laugh her mother stepped forward. 'Married to this oafish farmer? No, my darling, we can do better than that.'

She gripped Sophie's arm, and at her touch it all came back.

She was ten. She was in her bedroom and the night candle had gone out and she couldn't sleep and she was afraid. She didn't dare go to her mother because she'd been sent to bed early and that man was here again. He had a blue coat with lots of gold braid across the front, and he made her mother laugh and act silly. He always came when her father was away. Sophie didn't like him one bit.

Father was away hunting. He would be away all night in his hunting lodge in the woods. She was glad he wasn't there, because he filled the house with noise and drink and his red-faced friends and their women. Once, she and her mother had had fun when he was away, but now that man was always here.

Sophie longed for her mother. She crept out of bed and padded down the stairs and along the corridor to her mother's chamber on the first floor. When she got there, she heard voices within. Her mother wasn't alone! She pressed her ear to the door. That man was in there with her!

As she was wondering what to do, there was a huge bang. She spun around. There, by the front door, a lantern in his hand, stood her father.

'Wife!' he roared. 'Where are you?'

He sounded furious. He sounded drunk. Sophie darted away back into the shadows as he ran up the stairs and flung open her mother's door.

He let out a roar of rage.

Her mother screamed.

Heart racing, Sophie peered around the door, praying she wouldn't be seen. Her mother was in bed, the bedclothes pulled up, tears streaking her face, and that man was standing there, naked, backing away from the bed as her father advanced.

Her father slapped him across the face, and he stumbled. Then, suddenly, the man had a sword in his hand, was thrusting it forward and then there was blood everywhere and her mother was screaming and her father was falling to the floor.

Sophie fled back into the shadows by the stair to her nursery. She didn't know what to do. Then her mother's door burst open, and in the light pooling from it Sophie saw her mother and that man run down the stairs clutching bundles.

At the bottom of the stairs, her mother turned and stared up. Sophie was sure she was looking straight at her. Her first instinct was to run to her, but something in her mother's face stopped her.

The memory released her, and she fell back into the present, her mother's hand like a vice on her arm. The same dark expression was in her mother's face.

Sophie cried out, 'I won't go!'

Martin stepped forward to protect her, but then two men in footmen's livery ran into the room. One of them raised a pistol. There was a bang, a flash of smoke and Martin crumpled and fell. A spreading red stain on his chest.

Numb, she didn't resist as her mother pulled her away. She was bundled out of the house and into a waiting carriage.

Her mother was speaking, but Sophie barely heard the words.

'It has to be this way, my darling. I couldn't let you tell.'

All she could see were Martin's eyes staring blankly up at her. Her father's body falling to the floor.

Her mother pressed a cup into her hands and, automatically, she drank. Rich wine slid down her throat, but there was a bitter aftertaste.

The cup fell to the carriage floor and she stared at her mother with dawning horror. Sophie realised what she'd meant. She couldn't be allowed to tell. Her father and now Martin had been murdered, and Sophie had seen it. Now she was nearly of age, able to tell …

Then there was nothing but darkness.

The servants raised the hue and cry and told Mr van Heythuysen that his tenant had been snatched away. A man of integrity, he hired men to search for Sophie and the woman who'd murdered Martin Bull, but they found nothing.

No one wanted to rent the house. Everyone knew of the murder and disappearance, and people started to say the house was haunted. Lights were seen, and a white face would appear at the windows. The sounds of that ghostly hunt in the fields late at night were heard more often – just as they had been after the murder of the squire, all those years ago.

One day in 1772, a letter arrived from one of the agents van Heythuysen had hired. He'd been doing business in Belgium, delivering goods to a nunnery in Namur. The nuns had kept him waiting, so to while away the time he had wandered into their tranquil cemetery. Idly reading the gravestones, he ground to a halt when he saw a name he recognised. It was Sophie, and the date of death was just days after she'd been taken from Oulton.

The nuns were only too pleased to tell him what had happened. One night a carriage had rolled up in the dead of night, and a woman, seemingly wracked with grief, got out and explained that her daughter had been taken ill just outside the town and had died. She begged that they give her a Christian burial; she had money to pay. The nuns were all sympathy, but no sooner was the body brought in, the money given and the girl's name written down than the carriage was away! Of course they buried her, but they noticed something strange about the corpse. The girl had been dead for days, the old nun said, and they were sure she hadn't died naturally.

Upon reading this, van Heythuysen decided enough was enough. When Thomas Anquish of Lowestoft approached him about the house, he was all too happy to sell and forget about the whole sad business.

The house passed through many hands before ending up a conference venue in the 1980s. All those who lived there spoke of strange noises, of footsteps running down the stairs, and of a white face in the window.

That night, as Del and Tony sped back to Lowestoft, Oulton High House sat in darkness once more, but, if there had been anyone to see, they would have seen a white face pressed against a window upstairs, and heard in night the faint sound of a hunting horn and the baying of hounds …

19

Newmarket Legends

Fred Archer bent low over his horse's neck, feeling the wind in his hair. Beneath him Scotch Pearl felt as light as air, just as he did. There's nothing finer, he thought, than a gallop across the Severals on his favourite mount. Slowing, he turned on to Snailwell Road and trotted back to his stable yard with its distinctive clock turret. The horses being led through raised their heads, and the grooms struggled to control them. The dogs, too, looked up and their tails started wagging.

The people, on the other hand, ignored him, although they shivered as if a chill breeze blew as he rode past.

Fred felt pleased. He'd built these stables in 1882 and named them Falmouth Lodge. It'd been his dream to have his own stables to train in. He looked beyond them to the grand house he'd built for his wife and children. They were waiting for him.

He was eleven years old when his father, once a jockey himself, had sent him from their home at Prestbury, near Cheltenham's famous racecourse, to train with Mathew Dawson at Heath House stables here in Newmarket. He'd only been a young lad, but his dad and Dawson had seen he had talent. The Dawsons were kind; they took him to their hearts.

Winning races thrilled him. When that started happening he got the racing bug. He made up his mind to be the best jockey in the world – and to make plenty of money into the bargain. He'd had his eye on that prize all his life. They called him the 'Tin Man' – for all the tin, the lucre, he made! But there was a fly in the ointment. A successful jockey has to be small and light. Fred grew to five foot ten. He battled constantly to keep his weight down. He hardly ate, and made liberal use of Mrs Dawson's special purgative. It was hard, but it worked. His name was on everyone's lips, wealthy patrons sought him out and the money came rolling in. His success on the course was matched by his happiness in marrying Helen, Mat Dawson's niece.

Fred shifted in the saddle, remembering Helen. She'd been waiting for him a long time. Scotch Pearl shook her head, no doubt sensing his change of mood. With a last look around at the bustling stables, Fred let himself fade away.

The people in the big crowd of visitors in front of the stable block were still shivering, but the day's warmth began to return. The tall man at the centre of the group had noticed the animals' reactions a moment before. 'You here again, Fred?' he murmured under his breath, then turned back to the group to continue leading their tour.

A couple of the visitors, Josh and Caro, felt particularly thrilled to be at Pegasus Stables. They'd always promised themselves a trip to Newmarket, and this Open Day had been the ideal time to come. They were keen race goers, and, coming from Cheltenham, they'd long known about Fred Archer. They'd visited the hard to find cottage in Cheltenham where he was born and the King's Arms in Prestbury, where he'd grown up. They'd stood in front of the evocative print in the Cheltenham museum of Fred Archer's ghost galloping across the heath at Newmarket on his favourite grey horse, Scotch Pearl.

So, when Josh got a raise at work, they'd booked a week in Suffolk, stowed the bikes on top of the car and now were ensconced in a holiday cottage at Kentford. They glanced at each other and grinned. Here they were, in Fred's stables. They could feel his presence all around them as the owner continued Fred's story …

'It all seemed to be going perfectly. Fred was now in partnership with Mat Dawson, he was wealthy, popular, winning well and his wife was expecting their first child. But when he was only twenty-six

tragedy struck. His brother, a jockey in Cheltenham, was killed in a riding accident, and while Fred was still reeling from that, his newborn son died. Helen was soon pregnant again, and at the end of 1884 she gave birth to a healthy daughter; but their joy was cut short by Helen's sudden death a few days later.

'Fred never really recovered from this. The only thing that kept him going was winning. He starved himself even more. But his form began to wobble. He failed to win some important races. Unkind souls whispered that he was involved in race fixing and in gambling indiscretions. He admitted for the first time that he was unwell, but the call of the course drove him on. In a desperate bid to win for a prestigious patron he travelled to Sussex, but he returned home, the race unrun, in a state of collapse. He'd contracted typhoid. In his delirium and grief, he shot himself on 8 November 1886. He was twenty-nine.

'If you want to see Fred's grave, he lies with his wife and baby son in the cemetery up the other end of town. But,' – the owner paused for effect – 'we're sure his spirit is still here, at Pegasus Stables.'

Josh and Caro listened, spellbound.

'We try to run the place in a way that would make him proud. Let's show you how we've restored the original stables ...'

The owner showed them the innovative Victorian feeding technology inside the stable block, then led them away to the newer part of the stables.

'Where's his house?' someone asked.

The owner gestured over at the bungalows behind the stable. 'I'm afraid it was demolished back in the 1960s.'

After the tour Josh and Caro cycled out to see Fred's grave. Caro laid some flowers below the imposing cross.

'That's it then,' laughed Josh. 'We've seen where Fred was born, where he lived, where he worked and where he's buried.'

They finished their day with a stroll across the Severals. Next to the green where they walked was an exercise area with circuits marked out by white fencing, but seemingly empty of horses. Then they spotted at the back, a man on a grey horse galloping across the grass. It struck both Josh and Caro that the horse's feet didn't quite touch the ground. Caro shivered, wondering why that seemed so familiar.

Cheltenham came to mind, but at first she couldn't think why. Then she remembered – the print in the museum, showing Fred's ghost!

She turned to Josh to tell him, but he was staring at the exercise ground in confusion. The horse and rider had vanished.

'I think it's time to head back to Kentford,' he said, looking rather pale. 'I really fancy a pint.'

The guidebook told them that their route home took the road that was once the Icknield Way. They had to stop at a crossroads, and as they waited for a tractor to turn Caro spotted something on the other side of the road.

'What's that over there? It looks like a grave!'

Josh cycled over, then beckoned to her. 'You're right.'

They looked down at the little plot surrounded by a wire fence. Inside were tiny toy sheep, plastic flowers, lots of coins – and a cross with something written on it.

Josh read, 'Joseph, an unknown Gypsy Boy.'

That evening in the pub they asked about it.

An elderly man sitting at the bar spoke up: 'Thas allus called the Gypsy Boy's grave. Mebbe he were a Gypsy lad or just a little old boy what was working hereabouts. Anyways, it were more'n a hunner year ago. Whoever he were, they do say he were looking after some sheep for the farmer when one went missing. He were that frit o' bein' in trouble and likely his family too, that he hanged hisself from a tree.

He were found next morning and so was the missing sheep huddlin' in the ditch. Poor lad, on account of him having taken his own life he couldn't be put in the churchyard so they buried him right there at the crossroads. Thas allus bin kept tidy all this time. Some say 'tis the Traveller folk that dress it up. They say them ribbons'll tell you the colours of a winning horse. Lots of folk put things there for luck. It was a lady from London way what thought up the name Joseph and put the cross there. Thas got its secrets what we'll never know.'

In their cottage that night Josh poured them each a glass of Baileys.

'Let's drink a toast,' he said. 'We've seen two graves today and both were suicides. But how different they are – one a grand monument in a churchyard and the other a roadside memorial – but both still remembered.'

Caro raised her glass and they drank to Fred Archer and to the Gypsy Boy.

20

The Mill Cat

'But I don't *want* her to be dead!'

'There, there,' cooed Ralph's mother as she mopped his tears. 'Puss lived a fine, long life. It was God's plan to take her when he did. Now, shush, this is important, and if you can't be quiet, you'll have to go down.'

Ralph, his mother, father and three big sisters were all up in the loft of the mill. It smelt of freshly cut wood, and the sunlight from the open hoist door caught the motes of dust dancing across the room. Ralph knew his father was very proud of the new mill buildings. He'd taken Ralph outside and told him that one day it would all be his. Ralph was only seven, but he'd felt proud that day.

Then Puss had died. It had been Ralph who found her, curled up on her bed among the flour sacks. He couldn't remember a time when Puss hadn't been his friend. She strode around beside him and would always let him touch her kittens first, before any of his sisters. When he'd run, sobbing, with the cat in his arms to tell his mother, she'd comforted him, but then she'd taken Puss from him and said Puss would have a new job now.

His father had cut a hole in a beam in the loft, and now here they were, with poor Puss lying on the floor in front of them, looking pitifully small. Ralph began to cry again, but willed himself to be silent.

His mother gathered up Puss's body and carefully placed it in the hole.

'Loyal Puss,' she said, 'you served the mill well these ten years, catching mice and rats, and now you'll serve us again. Guard us, Puss. Keep the mill safe from evil, from fire and witches and flood and theft – especially fire, Puss; especially fire.'

Ralph's father plastered up the hole, and everyone trooped back down the ladder. Except Ralph. He went and placed his hand over the fresh plaster and whispered, 'I'll not forget you, Puss, I promise.'

Ralph kept his promise, even though one of Puss's sons, Gib, became his new friend. Ralph would often creep up to the loft and whisper his secrets to her. It was in her he confided when his parents refused his first choice of bride; to her he wept at his father's death. He brought all his sons and daughters to meet Puss, and told them of the good work she did, keeping fire and theft away from the mill. They carried on the tradition, starting when his own eldest son came up to tell Puss that old Ralph had died.

Over the years many people came up to the loft. Workers hauling out bags of flour to the waiting carts and boats. The miller catching a five-minute break. His children darting around the slanting beams and laughing. Maids and apprentices stealing kisses.

As the years passed into centuries Puss soaked it all in. She became part of the mill, and the mill became part of her. Not once in that time did fire damage the mill.

Sudbury Mill closed its doors for the last time in 1964. For seven years it sat derelict, and Puss's only company were the pigeons that roosted in her loft, but in 1971 that all changed. The new owners planned that the old flour mill by the Stour would buzz with people once more. The beautiful old building was to become an up-to-the-minute modern hotel.

There was a lot to do. The chimney had to come down. Extensions had to be built to house all the rooms. But they wanted the rest of the building to show its industrial heritage: the wheel would be taking pride of place in the hotel bar.

At first, the works went well. Then, one day, one of the partners heard a yell from the oldest, most precious, weather-boarded section of the mill. Up the ladders he hared, and, on clambering into the loft, he saw the builders clustered in a corner.

'What's wrong?'

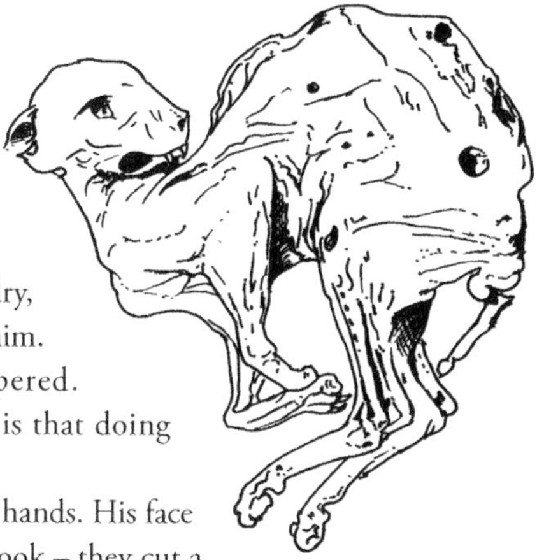

The foreman stepped forward, nervously fiddling with his moustache.

'We were just checking the beams, when John knocked one, and – look!'

Lying on the floor, was a white, dry, desiccated thing. It grimaced up at him.

'A mummified cat?' he whispered. 'Sweet Jesus, what in God's name is that doing there?'

John twisted his beanie hat in his hands. His face was ashen. 'It's barbaric,' he said. 'Look – they cut a special hole in the beam and plastered it in. Who'd do that to a poor kitty cat? That's evil, that is.'

It certainly gave the partner the creeps. Curled up like that, it looked as if it was hissing at some unseen enemy. He shook himself. It must have been the dust motes in the air. There was no way he could have seen a twinkle in the cat's eye.

'Just get it out of here,' he said, and headed back down the ladder.

Nobody wanted to touch it, so it was gingerly scooped up with a plastic bag and the foreman carried it off to dump it. But when he stood before the skip he found he couldn't. It was as if he could see that eye staring back at him. Before he knew what he was doing, he took it home. After all, it was a curiosity.

He had a group of friends round that night. When the Beaujolais had flowed long enough, he got the cat out.

'Why on earth have you brought that here?' cried his wife. 'I won't be able to sleep with that foul thing in the house!'

But an artist friend was fascinated. 'They were good luck charms, you know. Put there to protect against witches and the like.'

The foreman could see his wife wasn't having it, so at the end of the evening he popped the cat into a box and gave it to the artist.

Once he'd got it home, the artist wasn't sure what to do with it. Remembering the mummified cat he'd seen in the Nutshell, in Bury, he strung it up from the roof of his studio.

Back at the mill, the owners gave no thought to the cat, but within three months of the cat being found they ran out of money. Building work stopped and the mill once more lay silent and empty.

The wind blew through the hole in the beam in the roof … and a breeze stirred in the artist's studio, ruffling the papers, the cat rocking slightly on the strings that held it. Once there had been the murmuring of people, the clank of machinery, the singing of birds. Something was wrong. She could sense it.

This was the wrong place.

At first the artist had thought nothing of the cat hanging there among his other treasures, but the longer the thing was there the more malevolent it seemed. As he worked it seemed to always be facing around to stare right at him.

'It's like there's only room for it or my muse in here,' he muttered to himself, and he took the cat down and packed her up in a box and put her in the attic.

There was, at first, a sense of coming home. Hidden in the darkness, up high in a loft … But it wasn't the right place. It was wrong, all wrong. She knew it in her bones, in her crackly skin. Words fluttered through the empty skull. Something about fire?

'Spit spat,' said the cat.

Flames leapt into the Sudbury sky that night. There wasn't much the fire brigade could do. The place was gutted. The artist wept when he saw the ruination of his work, the canvases dripping with black, ashy water.

One of the firemen stepped forward, something in his arms. 'We saved what we could.' He held out a box.

With a sinking feeling the artist opened the box. There, unharmed, was the cat.

'It's a miracle,' said the fireman. 'Not a mark on it! I'm not a superstitious man, but that must mean something.'

The artist looked at the cat. Was that a spark he saw in its eye? He shuddered. 'Mean something'? That the thing was evil, he was sure.

He couldn't bear to keep it, but he didn't dare destroy it. God knows what would happen if he tried! The fire would be nothing in comparison. But some friends of his answered his prayers. They were restoring an old farmhouse in Wickham St Paul and, despite the artist's warnings, were keen to take the cat.

'It probably just misses its snug home. We'll find a wall space for it, and it'll be happy enough. It'll bring us good luck.'

Out in the village, the cat felt the pull of Sudbury more strongly. The longing for home pulsed through the dry skin. This was wrong.

'Spit, spat,' said the cat.

And in Wickham St Paul the fires leapt in the sky and the owners of the cottage watched their renovation crackle and spit ... and once more the cat was brought from the wreckage unscathed.

So the farm owner rang the artist, who rang the foreman, who took the cat back to Sudbury.

By now, new owners had taken on the mill project and the work was nearing completion.

The cat, stuck in her charred box in the foreman's house, sensed that something had changed, but things weren't right. This was not the mill. This was not her home.

'Spit, spat,' she said.

That night the roof of the mill collapsed. When the builders were allowed back in, they discovered that a beam had cracked in two, bringing the roof down and smashing through to the floor below. The foreman couldn't help but notice that the beam that'd cracked was the one in which the cat had been found. It was true that that beam had been weaker than all the others, thanks to the hole in it, but the foreman felt sure there was another explanation.

Acutely embarrassed, he went to the new owners and explained about the cat and all that had happened in the four years since it'd been found. To his surprise, the owners were prepared to listen. A board meeting was held, and all were in agreement. The cat had to come back to the mill.

A little grave was dug, the vicar of St Gregory's up the road was brought in and the cat was laid to rest with a note of apology.

After that, the building work seemed to go on like a dream. It finished ahead of schedule, and the Mill Hotel was ready to open.

The opening party was on 15 November 1975. The great and the good of Sudbury gathered to drink champagne and eat cheese and pineapple on sticks. After all the speeches, as people began to disperse, one of the owners cleared his throat.

'We've got one last thank you. It is with great pleasure that I welcome back our oldest resident!'

He pulled back a drape to reveal a hand-painted wooden sign, and then, while everyone was straining to read the words, he whipped away some fabric from the floor.

There were gasps, and he smiled at the suddenly fixed faces of the people.

'It was thought at first that she'd like a new home elsewhere, but you know how cats will walk hundreds of miles to find their way home … well, it seems that even long-dead ones crave their home comforts! So, we've made her a nice new home, in pride of place, and we fully expect her to resume her good work of keeping the Mill safe. Ladies and gentlemen, I give you … the luck of the Mill! Woe betide anyone who tries to take her out again!'

He smiled down at the little white form of the cat nestled in its new velvet bed. Just for a moment it seemed as if the cat grinned back.

21

Kate's Parlour

Jack Goddard was a butcher by day, but by night he was an entomologist. That summer's night, he and his friend Sidney headed down from Lowestoft to Jay's Hill, a lane between Sotterley and Hulver Street, for an evening's moth-catching. Sidney went through a gap in the hedge at the bottom of the hill, while Jack set up his lamp and white sheet at the top, near the Sotterley Hall's gate cottage.

Jack had sat there some time, an hour, maybe more, watching the moths fluttering around the light, when he suddenly heard horse's hooves pounding down the hill. He glanced at his pocket watch. It was past midnight. Thinking it strange that traffic should be coming by so late – and so fast – he quickly bundled up his moths in the sheet and, lamp in hand, waded back through the undergrowth.

The lane was empty. Jack stepped on to the road to have a look – and immediately felt a gust of hot strawy breath in his face and heard a terrified whinny echo through the empty air.

Shaken, he headed down the hill to see if Sidney had seen anything. Through the gap in the trees, he could see him still sitting staring at his moths. As Jack stepped through to join him a sudden chill passed through him and, turning, he caught a fleeting glimpse of something white in the road before it vanished.

Sidney waved him over. He was so clearly oblivious that Jack felt shy asking him if he'd seen – or heard – anything.

His friend shook his head. 'It was all quiet until you came crashing in.'

Jack didn't tell him what he'd seen, but the incident stayed with him.

A few weeks later he was back in the area, now in the safety of the

Hulver Gate. After a pint or two had slid down his throat, he felt emboldened to speak of his experience down the hill. There were knowing glances around the room.

'Kate's Parlour,' said George King. 'Thas a rum ol' place, and it were a rum do that made it so.'

The landlord, Albert Crane, a Norwich man who'd arrived a couple of years back in 1910, leaned over the counter. 'I've seen that on the map. Who's this Kate, then?'

'She knocked me off my bike, once,' said George. 'I'd just started to cycle up the hill, and, at the gap, there was a rush of wind. I saw something white, and there, right in front of me in the road was a woman dressed all in white, glaring at me. Well, I swerved, and ended up in the ditch, and when I picked meself up, there was nobody there! I'll not go that way again, not for anyone.'

'The hedge never grows there,' said young Eveline Antis. 'That's where they buried her. Her bones keep the trees from growing, see, cos she's still so angry!'

So it really was a ghost, Jack thought.

'But, who was she?' he asked. 'Why's she buried there?'

Kate was a Dunwich girl, a fisherman's daughter, growing up with salt breezes in her golden hair in the shadow of the half-ruined church of All Saints. By the end of the eighteenth century, the village was so small it no longer had a rector, so the children grew up half wild. Kate's mother made sure she learnt her letters and looked presentable. She was lucky; at the age of ten she was noticed by the Barne family, who owned Dunwich, and spirited away to begin a new life as a maid up at Sotterley Hall.

As she was a pretty girl, all golden curls and blue eyes, and because she was quick and bright, by the time she was seventeen she was a parlourmaid, waiting at table for Sotterley's gentlefolk. It was a big family, with all the generations in evidence, from the old brothers Miles, Barne, Snowdon and Michael to Michael's young children. Not just them; other scions of the family lived there, including two not much older than Kate, brothers Hugh and Piers. With so many gentlemen in the family, and the women mostly married away, it was no surprise that hunting and shooting were important in the Barne household. The family had a shooting box at Dunwich, and Kate was so well thought of that by the time she was twenty she would often go there with the family as acting housekeeper.

The little house was near the old Greyfriars ruins, in the woods on the cliff top. Kate loved going out there, inhaling the sea air and, though her parents were dead, there were old friends to visit when she could be released from her duties.

Two of the most frequent visitors to the shooting box were Hugh and Piers. Dunwich was a place where they could let their hair down. They would race about on their hunters over the gorse and the heather. They would track through the woods with their beaters, shooting down the fowl bred in the coverts.

Of the two, Piers was the quieter. Sometimes he would stay in the house, reading a book or writing letters, and he was not oblivious of the golden-haired young maid in the house with him. The inevitable happened. Something sparked between them. They couldn't help themselves. In secret they would steal out through the wood to the cliff. Feet dangling over the edge, Kate would regale Piers with stories from her childhood and he would tell her of Dunwich's history as a great city of fifty churches. Together they'd listen to see if they could hear the bells still ringing beneath the sea.

Perhaps if it had stayed just walks, all would have been well, but it did not. They were young, and Piers began to convince himself that since he was a younger son, unlikely to inherit much at all, no one would care who he married, so why couldn't he marry Kate? He declared that they were as good as engaged. He swore he would speak with his brother and all would be well. Even if Kate didn't quite believe it, she wanted to, so badly. The two of them lay down among the bluebells and gave each other their love, time and again.

Piers was as good as his word and went straight to his brother.

Hugh was horrified.

'A servant girl?' he cried. 'Are you a complete fool? You know we have little money of our own. You must marry well!'

He brushed aside Piers' declarations of love.

'Imagine what Miles would say, or Barne, or Michael! No, Piers, it cannot be.'

To ensure his brother thought no more of the girl, Hugh arranged straight away that Piers should go to town to study law. Before he could see Kate again, Piers was on a stagecoach to London.

For all his hard words, Hugh said nothing to anyone about the liaison, knowing that if he did, Kate would lose her position. Sure that his brother was the instigator, he kept quiet and hoped that everyone would soon forget the whole thing.

But as spring rolled into summer Kate discovered that she would never be allowed to forget, for, even if Piers seemed to have forgotten about her, he had given her something to remember him by. Not knowing where he had been sent, she could not send him word. Bitter were the tears she wept as the days warmed and the sun shone.

She managed to disguise the sickness well enough. She hid her despair and her weeping. But, by the end of the July when she studied her reflection in a mirror she knew she couldn't disguise her situation any longer. Even tightening her stays now hardly concealed the growing child in her belly.

She was right. The housekeeper, her friend for many years, finally noticed what had been under her nose for months. Kate was dismissed and told to leave with immediate effect.

Numbly she climbed the stairs to her room on the second floor and began to pack her few belongings. As she mechanically folded her dresses the numbness bled into anger. How dare Piers leave her all alone? Had he not loved her at all? Shame on the Barne family! This child is one of yours! Furious, she stripped off her maid's outfit – that wasn't hers to keep – and, clad just in her white shift, ran down the stairs to Hugh's study.

Hugh started when she came in. 'Kate! What are you doing?'

She stopped in front of him and drew the fabric of her shift tight across her belly to show him.

'You know this is Piers' child,' she said. 'You sent him away. Now you bring him back and let him marry me!'

For an instant she saw shame flit across his face, then it was gone.

'I know nothing of the sort,' he said. 'How dare you try and foist some stablehand or whatnot's child on my brother?'

The words were like a slap.

Stiffly she said, 'I have lain with no other man, I swear it. Piers said we would be married …'

Hugh turned from her and she saw him writing furiously.

'Look, take this.' He thrust a cheque into her hands. 'Now go. My brother has no desire to see you again.'

Kate stared at the cheque for a few moments. It was generous, and for a second she considered taking it. But, no, if this was what the Barne family thought of her, she'd have none of them! She ripped the cheque in two, then ran from the room.

Back in her room the enormity of her situation hit her. No husband, no father for her child, no job, not even any parents to run back to, if she'd dared. She was utterly ruined. There was nothing for her or this cursed child in this life any more.

At that moment the housekeeper came in.

'Why are you still here?' she cried. 'Get out, you hussy!'

Kate stared at her, hardly taking in the words. She turned to the open window and, without hesitating, flung herself out.

As a suicide, Kate couldn't be buried in the churchyard. Hugh arranged for her to be buried by the road at the bottom of Jay's Hill, close to the Hall that been her home.

He wrote a painful letter to Piers.

Piers was home in an instant. He wept and wept when he was told what had happened.

'I'd've married her at once, if only I'd known,' he whispered. 'To hell with the lot of you!'

Hugh blamed himself. Eventually, he persuaded Piers that they should go out for a drink to seek reconciliation. They both drank and drank that night. Piers was so angry; many hard words were spoken. On the way back, he pushed the horse that drew their trap faster and faster. When they came to Jay's Hill he realised that this was where his love was buried and he pushed the horse even more. Down the hill they raced.

From out of the woods suddenly shot something white, coming fast across the road towards them, a woman, her feet not touching the ground.

'Kate!' cried Piers.

The horse gave a terrified whinny as it felt something cold rush straight through it, and it skidded. The two young men were flung to the road, and in that moment came another vehicle, a horse and heavy cart, also going like the clappers down the steep hill. The driver saw them, he tried to stop, but he was going too fast. His horse and the cart ran straight over them both.

'And that night was the very same date you heard the horse,' cried George triumphantly.

'So Kate had her revenge,' said Jack, shaking his head.

He went away more unsettled than he'd come.

The following summer he took his family to Dunwich to play on the beach. They walked up to the tower of All Saints to marvel at how it teetered on the cliff edge. It put Jack in mind of Kate's sorrowful tale. When his children started to wilt and his wife suggested they go back, Jack walked on, into the wood. Ahead, through the trees, he could see the turrets of Grey Friars house beyond, but the wood was empty and silent.

From out of nowhere a figure appeared, walking away from him. With a sudden sense of dislocation, Jack realised that the man was dressed in the britches and long-tailed coat of a hundred years before. Worse was the sudden crushing melancholy that came over him and pinned him to the spot. Moments later, the figure vanished.

He ran back down to the beach where his family were playing, but said nothing. That night, he took himself straight off to the Hulver Gate. His friends greeted him with delight, but they quickly sobered when he told his tale.

'Thas wholly roight,' said George. 'They say Piers walks Greyfriars Wood where once he and Kate were so happy – and Hugh rides his horse over Dunwich Heath. But Kate still keeps to her windy parlour, and she's still unforgiving, even after so long.'

22

THE MAYFLY

That 23 June had been a busy day at the Wherry Hotel on Oulton Broad. The fine weather meant that all the tables in the bar and on the terrace were full at lunchtime. Then the wedding party had arrived mid-afternoon, noisy and happy in their flashy clothes. The bride and groom were finally waved away about eleven but the celebrations went on for another hour. By half twelve the weary staff had cleared up the worst of the debris. The cleaners could do the rest in the morning.

'I'm just nipping out for a quick fag, Paul,' said Mark. 'You coming?'

The two waiters walked down to the water's edge. The night was warm and calm, and there still seemed to be a glow in the sky, shimmering on the surface of the Broad.

'Phew,' said Mark, pulling a face. 'What an odd smell! What're they burning?'

'Yeah, smells ghastly,' replied Paul. He spotted a movement on the Broad. 'Look, there's a boat coming through.'

'Blimey, it's going like the clappers,' said Mark. 'What's it doing out this time of night?'

The vessel flew across the water, its great black sail taut and full. The hull had a strange sulphurous glow, and swirls of greenish yellow mist floated across the water.

As Mark and Paul stood transfixed, two figures appeared on the deck, waving their arms. Their faint cries carried across the water, but soon the wherry had reached the dyke and disappeared from view.

Mark stared up the Broad after the boat. 'Blimey, that was weird,' he said. 'Like watching a film, like it wasn't really there ... or something. You all right, mate?'

Paul's hands shook as he lit another cigarette.

'Not really, no. It's like we were seeing a ghost.'

'You know what,' Mark said slowly. 'That reminds me of something my grandad told me once, about a ghostly wherry ...'

Young Bert was nearly twelve, the eldest of six children. His ma and pa couldn't afford for him to be at home much longer. Pa worked long hours at the warehouse on the wharf, but the pay wasn't enough to feed so many hungry mouths.

Growing up a stone's throw from Beccles quay, Bert loved to watch the craft coming and going, and he fancied a life on a wherry.

The *Mayfly* was his favourite, always trim, loaded with goods coming in and out of Yarmouth, her black sail always smart. She belonged to Mr Dorney, who owned the wharf and who, Pa said, paid his workers better than Pa's boss did. Bert'd chatted many times to Jack and Tom, the *Mayfly*'s regular crew, so he'd thought he'd try his luck.

'That'll be hard graft, lad,' Jack said. 'You up to it, d'you reckon?'

In 1851, four years after Bert started, the *Mayfly* got a new skipper. All he, Jack and Tom knew about him was that his name was Stevenson and he'd not long arrived in Beccles. Stevenson decreed that the wherry needed a refit. She was smartened up with new paint and rig, and her sail was given a fresh dressing of herring oil and coal tar. So far, so good, but one morning Bert, Jack and Tom came down to find the tiller replaced by a wheel.

'Don't know what Mr Dorney's thinking of, taking on this bloke,' said Jack. 'But it's not up to us. If he knows his way around a boat then so be it.'

They found out from men who'd come across Stevenson in Yarmouth that he'd been on merchantmen for years, but he was a mean-looking cove, and handy with his fists. He'd won round Mr Dorney, but the crew soon grew to dislike him.

On the morning of 23 June they were called together.

'We've a special cargo this trip,' said Stevenson. 'Mr Dorney is shipping a chest of money to Yarmouth, and his daughter, Miss Millicent, is coming along to watch it. The story you're to say is that she's going to stay with her aunt in Yarmouth and the trunk is her baggage. Any word of the money and it'll be the worse for the lot of you.'

Bert winked at Jack, who had a soft spot for the boss's daughter, but quickly wiped the grin off his face when he caught a look from the skipper.

Miss Millicent, a slight, fair girl of eighteen, arrived with her father. Jack stepped up to help her on board, but Stevenson elbowed him aside and took her aft to the cuddy, the little cabin.

'This'll be your private quarters for the trip, Miss Dorney,' he said, all obsequious. 'If you need anything, don't hesitate to ask.'

On their familiar journey downriver they had a fair wind behind them. Either side of the Waveney were great tracts of marshland fringed with gently swaying willow and reeds. The sails of wind pumps turned ponderously. From Oulton Dyke the river swung north past Somerleyton and the Herringfleet Marshes. At St Olaves the New Cut swept away to Reedham but the *Mayfly* stuck to the old route to Burgh Castle and the Yare. Being midsummer, it was still light when they came through Breydon Water on the last stretch before Yarmouth.

'Take the wheel, Bert,' called the skipper. 'Jack, a word, if you please.'

As he steered Bert was startled to hear Jack call out: 'Never! It's not yours to take! And you shan't lay a hand on her!'

At that the skipper took hold of Jack's shirt, but Jack was swinging his fist. They traded blows by the mast, then with a mighty uppercut Stevenson sent Jack flying off the deck and into the water.

Bert yelled out and Tom came charging up from the hold.

'Jack's gone over!' shouted Bert, but when Tom ran to sling a rope the skipper blocked his way.

'Take the helm, Tom,' he ordered. 'Keep her steady.' Tom tried to speak, get past him, but the skipper said, 'You have your orders, sir!' Then, 'Bert, get below!'

As Bert fled to open a hatch, praying that Jack might swim to safety, the door to the cuddy opened and Miss Millicent's pale face looked out. 'Is everything all right?'

Bert opened his mouth, but Stevenson cut in: 'Couldn't be better, Miss.'

Bert peered out from under his hatch cover, and saw her bob back down. Stevenson and Tom were speaking, but he couldn't hear. He had to know what was going on, so, trembling, he crawled out from the hatch and inched his way back along the deck.

'You'll do as I say unless you want to end up like Jack.' The skipper's voice was quiet but menacing. 'I'm in charge of this tub and my orders are to steer for Rotterdam. That's final.'

With that he strode off along the starboard plankway.

Rotterdam! Bert was aghast. He crept further along, on his belly, and stuck his head round the corner of the cabin. He gave a low whistle and Tom turned. His face was drawn, his knuckles white on the wheel. He gave a small shake of his head.

Before Bert could speak, the door of the cuddy opened again and out came Miss Millicent.

'Are we nearly in Yarmouth, Tom?'

At the sound of her voice Stevenson reappeared. Bert flattened himself on the plankway. He was nearly at the wheel now.

'Captain, it's been a most comfortable trip,' said Miss Millicent. 'I can't thank you enough.'

'Oh, but I think you can. We're not putting in at Yarmouth. We're off to Rotterdam, you and me. Way I sees it, you're a fine lass, and so we'll be hitching up. That chest of money there, that'll set us up nicely. What d'you say, my pretty?'

With no clear idea what he was going to do, Bert jumped up. The same moment, Tom left the wheel and darted between Stevenson and the terrified girl.

'Get away, you villain!' he shouted.

Stevenson was quick. He threw his fist into Tom's face with such force that Tom staggered backwards and hit his head on the iron-bound gunwale. Bert dashed to help him but Stevenson grabbed his arm in a vice-like grip.

'Leave him!' he growled. 'Take the wheel or you'll be next.'

Stevenson turned to the weeping girl, huddled on the steps of the cuddy, then pushed her inside and slammed the door behind them.

Shaking, tasting vomit in his mouth, Bert disobeyed long enough to check Tom's still form. His friend's eyes stared past him, empty. Terrified, he returned to the wheel and lashed it. He lit the lamps as it was finally getting dark. They were entering Yarmouth, lights glinting on either side of the Yare. As he steered the vessel out from Southdown Quay he heard the midnight chimes. The North Sea lay ahead. Bert's mind raced. What should he do? If he tried to turn the boat or run her aground or do anything against the skipper's commands, he'd likely suffer Jack and Tom's fate. And there was the girl, ensconced with that monster. He'd have to stick it out and leg it when they next touched land.

The deck heaved under his feet and the sail boomed as the wind took it. Bert had never been on the open sea. He felt so helpless.

Then, a piercing scream from the cuddy. The door burst open and Miss Millicent threw herself almost at his feet. Her hands were clasped to her throat. In the lantern's light he saw blood seeping through her fingers. The skipper barrelled out after her, a blade flashing in his hand, and, before Bert could do anything, she rushed off for'ard, Stevenson in pursuit. Bert didn't stop to think. He lashed the wheel again and ran after them. In the gloom he saw Stevenson reach her, then one was down. He distinguished Miss Millicent clinging to the mast.

'Hold on, Miss, I'm coming,' Bert yelled as he crossed over the slippery hatches, dodging the swinging foot of the sail.

He found the skipper sprawled across the hatches by the mast. The girl was now on her knees beside him. Bert reached out to her but she toppled sideways and lay still, dark blood flowing from her neck.

Bert searched desperately for signs of life, but found none. The skipper's shirt was soaked red. In Miss Millicent's hand was a blood-stained knife.

Bert leaned his head against the mast. He was alone, at night, with three dead bodies on a boat not built for the open sea. The sail was bellying wildly. The *Mayfly* rose and dived at the mercy of the waves. He couldn't stay on board with the dead, and yet pitching them into the sea seemed wrong. It was him who'd have to go.

He grabbed a lantern and a flask of water, then gingerly climbed down into the dinghy, cut the rope and prayed as he had never prayed before.

'God rest you, Miss Millicent, Jack, Tom,' he called into the wind. 'And may you, Stevenson, rot in hell.'

How long he drifted he didn't know. Eventually there was a light, a vessel approaching. Bert jumped up shouting and frantically waving the lantern. As the object of his hopes drew near, the moon slipped from behind the clouds. Bert saw that this was no rescue ship. The *Mayfly* was sailing towards him, lit by an unearthly glow and wreathed with sulphurous smoke. She passed so close he could've touched her. The spectral figures of Stevenson and Miss Millicent ran round and round the deck. Was that Tom at the helm? No, it was Death himself, grinning down at him … Bert's knees failed under him, and all went black.

He awoke in a dry, clean bed.

'Where am I?' he whispered.

'Lowestoft Hospital,' said the young nurse. 'You've been here two weeks. A poor thing you were, raving and jabbering, when the mate from the trawler brought you in. You're a lucky lad.'

She brisked away, and the old sailor in the bed next to him said, 'You were just crying about a mayfly, and a Miss Millicent.'

At the mention of the word 'mayfly' it all came flooding back.

'Mr Dorney, I've got to tell Mr Dorney!'

The old sailor nodded, and in the face of his sympathy Bert told his tale.

As he spoke of the ghostly apparition the sailor's eyes took on a gleam: 'She be a death ship now, in the Devil's navy. She be cursed to sail and never make port till the trumpet calls her and wherever she goes death is in her wake, you mark my words.'

A week later Bert was in a carriage on his way back to Beccles. Mr Dorney himself had come for him. When Bert told him the awful tale, Mr Dorney wept. The loss of the wherry and the money was nothing to the loss of his daughter.

'I should never have sent her, never hired that man. And the families of those poor men, what am I to say to them?'

Bert wept with him, but he didn't tell of his terrifying vision in the dinghy.

Their shared grief created a bond between Bert and Mr Dorney. Mr Dorney kept Bert in his employ and they took to going fishing together of an evening along the Waveney. It was peaceful, no words needed. On the anniversary of the disaster, a few years later, the memories of the tragedy weighing heavy on their minds, they went to a favourite spot on Oulton Dyke.

Just gone midnight a mist came rolling in.

'I reckon we'd best be getting back, sir,' said Bert.

The mist smelt strong and almost choking. He heard sudden shouts in the distance and, looking up, saw a wherry coming from the direction of the Broad, sail full though there was little wind. A feeling of horror crept over Bert. The wherry's hull and mast were picked out by an eerie glow and around her swirled an evil-smelling vapour. As she drew abreast, Bert watched, transfixed, the two wraith-like figures moving on the deck.

A woman's voice cried out, 'Save me, Father, save me …'

Mr Dorney was on his feet. 'Milly? Is that you?'

Bert suddenly heard the old sailor's words echo in his mind: 'Wherever she goes death is in her wake …' He paled, gasping: 'Dear Christ, she's coming for me!'

The spectre sped past, the cries growing fainter, the glow fading into the mist. Bert drew a deep breath and turned. Mr Dorney no longer stood beside him. He lay still, hand clutching his chest. Bert had seen enough corpses to know he was gone.

I am cursed, thought Bert. Cursed to see that hell-boat and watch while others die.

'Is that what we just saw, then?' Paul stubbed out his cigarette and reached for another. 'A ghost ship? I've never believed in ghosts.'

'That's the tale my grandad told,' said Mark. 'Always said it was a cock-and-bull story. But it is the twenty-fourth of June, after all.'

'But what about how Mr Dorney died, though? Does someone die if you see it? Does that mean one of us will?' Paul's hand was shaking as he lifted his cigarette.

Mark gazed out over the water. 'Dunno,' he said. 'But if you don't cut down on those fags it just might.' He stood up. 'Come on, mate. Time to go home. Another busy day tomorrow – there's no peace for the wicked, eh?'

23

The Educating of Ellen de Freston

Lord de Freston doted on his only child, Ellen. After the loss of his wife and baby son, Ellen was everything to the lord. He lavished on her not only affection, but also education. The little girl was tutored in the arts of needlework, musicianship and painting. She was taught household management. Her father taught her, too, to respect his tenants and servants and to give to the poor. All of these were right and proper for a girl in the fifteenth century, but there was more. She learnt philosophy, literature, Latin and Greek. De Freston's friends said he was misguided. A girl's mind would be overheated by all this book learning. It would make her unmarriageable. He dismissed their concerns. The child was bright, but once she was a woman other interests would take the place of learning.

There was one thing missing. With no siblings to play with, the child dedicated all her time to her books. It wasn't healthy. Her love of learning was to be encouraged, but she needed friends. Lord de Freston came up with a plan: he would open up his house as a school for the brightest and the best. Any child, low or high, could come there for lessoning.

Soon, the house was filled with childish laughter. There were few lordlings here; instead there were the likes of Thomas Wolsey, an Ipswich butcher's son, and William Latimer, clerk's son and poor relation to the Latimers who owned the other half of the manor of Freston. There were girls, too, like Ellen not satisfied with sewing. De Freston laughed to see his charges down by the Orwell poking in the mud in the name of natural philosophising and to see them declaiming Cicero's speeches. His true reward was to see his daughter so bright-eyed and happy.

It pleased him when the children blossomed under his care. He decided to support some of the poorer boys in their next step, university. Unbeknownst to him, however, his daughter was growing up and realising that, though there was no difference between her intellect and that of the boys, her life would be very different. The first he knew of that was when she came to him in a fury.

'Why can't you send me to Oxford? I am surely as deserving as Thomas and William. I am your daughter!'

Lord de Freston felt the first faint stirrings of unease.

'Ellen, you are a bright child, so you know that this cannot be. It pleases me to see that my daughter is so curious and clever, but you know that you must marry. Girls cannot go to Oxford – or to Cambridge either.'

Ellen stamped her foot and ran to her room. He followed her, but her maidservant said that Ellen would not see him. He knew he should go in, enforce his will, but when he heard her sobbing beyond the closed door he turned away, feeling helpless.

Ellen said no more of this to him and threw herself back into her studies. But things were changing. One by one her friends left. The boys off to university and, worse, the girls getting married.

Soon, she was alone. Her father dismissed the tutors, saying that for one young girl it was too much. She said nothing, but continued her reading alongside her sewing and music-making. Letters came from Thomas and William at Oxford. Thomas said he was considering the Church. Her father noticed how Ellen looked thoughtful when she heard this. Another thread of unease ran through him. That evening she came to him and said, 'Father, I understand that I cannot go to Oxford, but there is a place where a woman can study, isn't there? Please, Father, I do not wish to marry. Let me go into a nunnery.'

He looked into his daughter's grave face and knew that his friends had been right to fear he would spoil the child with all that learning.

'That cannot be. You know you must marry. If you have no children the estate will be entailed and we will lose this land for ever.'

To see the light go out of her eyes grieved him, but she agreed to meet potential suitors. Lord de Freston's estate was rich and the men came flocking. They were very different from the boys Ellen had known. They laughed when she tried to talk philosophy with them, and called her 'charming' in mocking tones when she spoke Latin. Only when she sang and played did they praise her.

She refused them all.

Lord de Freston was furious. He had lavished all his love and care on her, but she had grown wilful and spoilt. Well, he would grant her wish to study – but she would rue the day she demanded it.

On the banks of the Orwell a strange structure began to grow. Bargeloads of brick were brought from Ipswich, and a precious load of stone came all the way from Caen in Normandy. The structure grew and grew until a tall tower stood beside the river.

Lord de Freston waited until it was complete, then he brought Ellen to it.

'This, my girl, is your new home. You wanted to study? Well, study you shall. Alone.'

He led her inside.

'On the ground floor you will meet the poor and give them alms.'

Up a flight of spiral stairs they went.

'Here you will sew and weave.'

On the second floor were her musical instruments.

On the third, wide windows flooded the tower with light. 'Your painting room.'

On the fourth were all her books. Lastly, he led her on to the roof, where the wind whipped their hair and clothes.

'Here you may study the stars. There is a telescope, an expensive thing. But you will go no further outside than this – until you consent to marry.'

The look in Ellen's eyes wounded him, but he knew he must persevere. He had been lax, and now she must suffer for his foolishness.

For months Ellen worked alone. She met with the poor and listened to their stories. She sewed, and played, and painted, and read. At night she would go up on the roof and gaze at the stars and chart their progress across the sky. She watched the changing moods of the river and saw the barges come and go from Ipswich. In summer she took her reading to the roof and trained her telescope on the barges to see people laughing and talking. Her heart ached with loneliness.

One day, she realised that she had nothing to do. She had read all the books, studied a year's worth of stars. She saw the rest of her life rolling out before her, trapping her with no more to do than the same things over and over. The walls of the tower seemed to close in around her. Up the stairs she ran, to the roof. The wind clawed at her hair and skirts as she rushed to the edge. For a moment she considered jumping, but she couldn't throw her soul away like that. She went back down the stairs and waited for her father's weekly visit.

'Father, I have exhausted all the tower can give me. I will stay here, if that is your will, but I beg you, give me tutors again, so that I may learn more.'

'Ellen, you must relent. You are twenty-one. All your friends are married with one or two little ones. You must see reason! There will be no tutors.'

Ellen did not speak, just turned and walked away back up the stairs.

The next he knew was that her servants came to tell him she would not eat.

He begged her to unbend, but she would not. As he watched her eyes grow dull, her body weaken, something snapped. What a fool he was! This was his beloved daughter! Why was he treating her like this?

He asked around, and when he heard that young William Latimer was back from Oxford, working as a clerk, he knew his prayers were answered.

Under William's tutelage Ellen soon recovered. She listened with bated breath as he told his tales of Oxford. She pored with delight over the new books he brought. Men on the passing barges would look up as laughter rang out from the once silent tower.

It seemed the ideal arrangement, but Lord de Freston had overlooked one crucial thing. He had seen Latimer as merely a tutor. His daughter saw him as a man. And William? How could he not fall in love with his old childhood friend, grown so clever and so fair?

Full of excitement, Ellen went to her father.

'We will do such good things together! We will found a school for boys and girls, we will teach the poor to read and write, so they may better themselves …'

Lord de Freston listened in bewilderment. Marry her tutor, a mere clerk's son? He would not have it! He forbade the union and banished Latimer back to Ipswich.

But Latimer had seen this coming and had planned for it. He knew he was no match for Ellen – as a poor lad at Oxford, he'd seen how the world worked – but he was not prepared to let Ellen go.

Three days Ellen stayed in the tower. Let her father believe she was sulking!

On the third day, late, a barge pulled up at the wharf below the tower. She watched as the crew loaded up and then settled down to spend the night in the boat.

Meanwhile, William Latimer was in Stoke, just south of the Orwell, with a pack on his back and a lantern in his hand, ducking down a set of steps that led underground. The tunnel was dank, and his feet sloshed through water, but he knew the tide times. He knew that smugglers used this route to get goods away without going through the tolls at the port in Ipswich. They'd dock at Freston, carry the goods through the tunnel to Stoke and be away upriver unseen.

He walked and walked until, at last, there were the rough steps upward. When he emerged in the darkness before dawn, a mist was already coming down. The tower loomed out of it, dark and silent.

Ellen was waiting by the door. Together they ran down to the wharf and as the darkness faded to the pearly greyness of a misty dawn the waiting boat was pulling away downriver to the sea.

The boat was spotted from the house before the mist swallowed it. Lord de Freston raced down to the wharf, calling for his daughter. But the barge was long gone. Up to the tower he ran, up the stairs, his heart racing, till he emerged into the mist on the roof.

'Ellen!' he cried. 'Come back!'

He called out until he was hoarse, his voice lost in the mist. There was no answering cry.

De Freston fell into deep grief. No word came from his daughter, but each day he would creak up the tower and watch the boats going by, calling out to each one for his daughter. No answer ever came. Before the year was out he was dead.

Ellen and William never returned. It was Lord de Freston's spirit that lingered.

On misty mornings on the river, sailors and bargees drifting along in the suffocating silence, working out their position by soundings and dead reckoning, would suddenly hear a voice. Thin, and distant, from across the still water, muffled by the fog.

'Ellen ...' the voice cried.

The sailors said the voice sounded old, tired, worn to a thread, but insistent. Some spoke too of how their boat would pull there, towards the shore, and it was all they could do to get it back on course.

Nowadays, it's rare for a boat to be out on the river in inclement conditions, but when the mist falls you can still hear that voice calling for a daughter who never returned.

24

The Haunting of Old Hall

The young postulants clustered around the heater, trying to stave off the winter's cold. Brother John was smiling at them in his slightly nervous way. His shock of white hair added years to a face that wasn't so old, even to these young men.

'During the war the lads used to tell ghost stories on nights like this,' he said, his eyes unfocused, as if he saw something they didn't. 'I never knew whether it made the nights longer or shorter.'

The postulants glanced at each other. They'd told their fair share of spooky stories when the brothers weren't around.

'I know one from Old Hall itself,' said John, his fey grin getting wider. 'Would you like to hear it?'

Many conscripted Shrewsbury lads ended up in the King's Shropshire Light Infantry back in the autumn of 1939. They were in for a surprise, though. Instead of heading off to war they were bound for the West Indies to guard Dutch oil refineries. Harry Purslow and Ted Lewis, who'd been mates since school, imagined an island paradise of sun, warm seas, tots of rum and dark exotic women. What more could a chap want? Their cabin-mate on the long voyage, Jack Price, viewed this prospect with trepidation. He was a nervous, skinny lad with round glasses and a shock of black hair. Harry and Ted had taken him under their wing. Someone had to, as he jumped at every shadow and was happiest with his nose buried in a book. Amazing he'd made the grade, really.

'The place is full of ghosts and evil spirits,' he'd say, pointing to a passage in his book. 'There's the Father of the Forest and his Devil Woman wife who hides behind trees waiting to lure men to their deaths.'

'Cut it out, Jack,' snapped Ted. 'You read too many books for your own good!'

Despite Jack's ongoing jumpiness and his alleged sightings of hoodoos, they had an easy time. Almost three years they were there, but all good things have to come to an end, don't they? Come 1942 they were on a ship back to Blighty.

Island life had not prepared them for the real world of soldiering, so they were off to a transit camp for some 'sorting out', as old Sergeant Crisp put it. No one was looking forward to it much, and it was a subdued bunch who travelled on the train to Manningtree, then into trucks for the short ride to some place called East Bergholt. Their destination turned out to be a great fortress of a place – Old Hall.

'Blimey, looks like a bleedin' prison,' Ted said to Harry and Jack as they marched in past the high forbidding walls.

Jack soon ferreted out that Old Hall had been a nunnery for nearly a century, but fear of invasion had sent the nuns packing and the army had moved in. The place was huge, all Victorian gothic and gloom. Not that they saw all of it. The chapel was locked for the duration.

'You're not getting in there, boys,' said Crispie. 'Too good for the likes of you!'

Harry, Ted and Jack were billeted together, in a cell that a nun must have once used.

'Those nuns must be turning in their graves, what with us lot here,' grinned Harry.

'Don't joke – it's creepy enough already,' said Ted. 'You know Jack swears he felt something down that passage to the back gate. Right weird he said it was, cold and clammy. He won't go that way now. Takes the long way round.'

'Here we go!' Harry scoffed. 'Remember what he was like overseas? It better not be hoodoos and devil women behind every tree here!'

Sergeant Crisp stuck his head round the door. 'Ain't you lads got work to do?'

He was looking a bit grey round the gills.

'You all right, Sarge?' asked Ted. 'You look like you've seen a ghost.'

Crispie scowled at him. 'Don't mock, boy. It's nothing we can't handle.'

'What's eating him?' Harry asked.

Jack edged into the room. 'It's the sergeants' mess,' he said, looking around furtively before going on. 'I heard there's been some odd goings-on in there lately and it's keeping them up at night.'

Harry dug Ted in the ribs. 'Never thought the sarge was that way inclined!'

Jack went red. 'It's nothing like that! They've got a ghost.'

'Bloomin' 'eck, Jack!' Ted rolled his eyes. 'What is it with you and ghosts?'

'This is real.' Jack's eyes were wide behind his glasses. 'Every night at the same time, ten to eleven on the dot, the door opens and a cold blast of air comes in.'

'And that's it?' said Harry. 'Come off it, Jack – this place is full of cold draughts. Don't half feel it after the Indies.'

'Well, they believe something's going on,' said Jack. 'They've put someone outside the door to check there's no one there and it still happens. They're going to take the door off tonight and see if that'll sort it.'

'Well, that's your department, Jack,' said Harry. 'Me, the only goose-bumps I want are those caused by seeing the Suffolk girls at the dance tonight. Got my eye on that Shirley Hicks, I have.'

Jack watched them get ready. The dances at the Hall had become a regular thing. The regimental band was pretty good, and the local girls came along for the fun. Harry joked that the lads weren't much cop at dancing – a lot of toes got trodden on. To him and Ted it was all a good laugh, and Jack could see it made them forget there was a war on – and the fact they'd soon be in the thick of it.

He was a bit envious of his friends, but he didn't fancy the dance. He always felt awkward. He preferred a book and an early night. After the evening meal he wandered back towards his billet. When he reached the sergeants' mess, there was Crispie with a screwdriver, taking the door off its hinges.

'Want a hand with that, Sarge?' offered Jack.

'Right you are, Price. Grab a hold there and we'll have it off in a jiffy.'

The job was soon done.

'Not off to the hop, Price?' asked Crispie.

'Not tonight, Sarge. Got a bit of a dicky ankle,' Jack lied.

Crispie's eyes gleamed. 'Tell you what, Price, seeing as you're available, I'm assigning you guard duty. With the door off, we might get any old riff-raff wandering in. Cup of cocoa in it for you. What d'you say?'

Jack had no desire to stay, but didn't feel he had any choice.

'I suppose so, Sarge. It won't be for long, will it?'

'You'll be all right, Price. Just keep your peepers open. See you at eleven.'

'Eleven?' Jack went pale. Didn't the ghost come at ten to eleven? He ran his hands through his thick black hair.

'Don't be a baby, lad,' said Crispie. 'And see you get that hair cut pronto.'

Then he was off, whistling loudly, leaving Jack alone.

Jack pulled up a chair and sat down in the doorway wishing he had a book with him. The hours ticked by so slowly. At a quarter to eleven he looked at his watch for the umpteenth time.

'Come on, Sarge. I really don't want to be here any longer,' he muttered.

He took his chair back into the mess room. Then, as he turned to leave, the temperature plummeted. A cold blast of air rushed through the open doorway. It hit Jack full in the chest, knocking his breath away.

'Bleedin' Nora, I'm out of here!'

He was bolting down the corridor as Sergeant Crisp came round the corner.

'Oi, Price, where do you think you're going?'

Jack skidded to a halt. 'It was the ghost, Sarge!' he cried. 'Ten to eleven, just like everyone says! Freezing cold it was!'

Crispie coughed and looked at his watch. 'Ghost, eh Price? Lot of, er, nonsense, if you ask me. Want that cocoa?'

'No thanks, Sarge.'

The sergeant hesitated, seemingly reluctant to go on to the mess room.

He coughed again. 'All right, Price, as you were.'

Jack scuttled back to his room and into his bunk. The lads'll be back soon, he thought as he burrowed under the blanket.

After a while he heard the door opening.

'That you, Harry? Ted?' he called.

The light from the corridor shone dimly in and seemed to waver in an odd sort of way. Jack reached for his glasses but they were still on his nose.

'You there, lads? Stop messing about!'

No one came, just seeping coldness. Jack lay pinned to his bunk in terror. He felt the chill surround him. Ice cold hands brushed his face. He screamed.

Meanwhile, Harry and Ted had been making their way back from the dance.

'Shirley's a great girl,' said Harry. 'She cycles over from Flatford, you know. Her dad's a farmer and she's been organising the land army girls who come to help out. Pity we'll be moving on soon. Still, you never know.' He sighed. 'What about you? I saw you cosying up to her friend Phyllis, reckon you're in there?'

They were laughing as they turned down the corridor past the sergeants' mess, where Crispie was hunched over his cocoa.

'Quiet night, Sarge?' asked Harry.

'So-so, boys. So-so. Your mate Price was here a while ago. Seems a bit on edge. You'd better see if he's all right.'

Then the night was split by a man's scream.

'What the flamin' 'eck's that?' cried Ted.

All three ran towards the sound. As they came to the corridor where their billet was, Harry and Ted saw that their door was open. They heard whimpering and sobbing from inside.

'Jack, Jack, you there? What's up, Jack?'

Ted flicked on the light, and Jack bolted up, his eyes full of fear.

'It was the ghost,' he said, his voice cracking. 'It came after me. I know you think I'm stupid but I felt it, I did, I tell you. But you won't believe me; you never do.'

The three men stared at Jack in amazement.

'It's all right, mate,' said Harry. 'We believe you. We believe you now.'

Jack sighed in relief, snow white hair flopping over his wide dark eyes.

The postulants all stared at Brother John as they took in his last words.

'Where was the mess, Brother?' asked one, trying to keep the quiver out of his voice.

John's eyes gleamed. 'I do believe it was right here.'

25

The Unlayable Ghost

'Why can't that stupid girl get it into her head what she needs to do?'

Farmer Underwood of Pakenham was furious. The girl had her instructions. You'd think that the clearing up would drum it into her tiny mind that if she – and everyone else – wanted a quiet life, then all she had to do was lay that extra place at the table. But no. He knew it was partly his fault for not spotting the place setting wasn't there. But it had been a long day out in the fields and the last thing he wanted to do when he got home was to calculate how many farmhands and servants would be joining them at table. That was the kitchen's job – and they weren't doing it!

He had sunk into his chair that night with a heartfelt groan. The lads were helping themselves and laughing. All he could think about was how good that ham looked and how fine his beer was going to taste.

Then, before his very eyes, the potatoes flew up into the air.

Everyone stopped and stared at the potatoes dancing above their heads, and they held their breath.

Bedlam ensued. The plates, the knives, the forks, up they all went. Food sprayed everywhere. The maid was shrieking. The farmhands were shouting. The dogs outside started howling.

Then Farmer Underwood's tankard shot

up above his head. The room went very still. He backed his chair away sharpish – but it was too late. The tankard tipped and a pint of foaming nut-brown ale poured on his head.

It was all getting too much, this living with a ghost.

'Well, my dear,' said his wife, 'isn't it time to get the parson in?'

That's how, next day, Farmer Underwood found himself sitting awkwardly in his best clothes in the parlour while his wife poured the tea and served up dainty cakes. The parson beamed at him, and asked how long this had been going on.

Farmer Underwood cleared his throat.

'The man who sold this place to us said it was the one as built it was the trouble. There was some kind of double dealing, something not quite right about how the builder'd got the money. I never got to the bottom of it, but the long and the short of it is that him as built this place never left. He was so troubled by what he'd done that he stayed, and he's been making our lives a misery ever since we came!'

'How does he manifest himself?' the parson asked.

The farmer's wife spoke up: 'He's everywhere, Reverend. In the kitchen he tips over the milk and the flour. He whips off the sheets when we're sleeping, and he tips the water from the jug! But it's at table he's the worst; the only way we can get around it is by laying an extra place – but now we'd rather lay him!'

The next day the parson arrived with his exorcism kit and started his prayers. The spirit was reluctant, so he had to pray all the harder. He chased the spirit out of the kitchen and into the parlour, it all the while knocking over tables and chairs, crashing pictures from the walls ... Up the stairs he chased it, praying hard all the way, until he'd cornered it in the fusty best bedroom.

Using all the power of prayer, his Bible clutched in his sweating hand, the parson forced the struggling spirit into a cupboard. It was the work of moments then for the farmer to seal the door and stop the lock.

'That's all we can do,' said the parson. 'He's locked up tightly in there. So long as you don't open that door, all will be well.'

Farmer Underwood did trust in the Lord, but he was also the kind of man who liked to tie up his camel. That afternoon he and his wife papered over that cupboard so that you'd never know it was there.

That night the farmer, his wife, the farmhands and maids sat gingerly down to dinner with no extra place laid. The potatoes stayed on the plates, the plates stayed on the table and, best of all, Farmer Underwood's ale stayed in his tankard until he came to drink it!

The farmer and his wife never had any children, so when they died a new family came all the way from Stowlangtoft to take on the farm. They knew nothing of the house, and the new farmer's wife fancied herself and her husband in the best bedroom, fusty though it was.

She scrubbed and cleaned, she wiped and mopped, and soon the room was as fresh as a daisy. But, as she was manhandling the cleaning equipment out of the room, she knocked into the wall and realised it was hollow.

It was the work of moments to strip off the wallpaper. Underneath was a perfectly useable cupboard. How strange, she thought. She had the lock unstopped and the frame unsealed. There was no key, but her husband jemmied it. A lick of paint was all that was needed to freshen up the cupboard before she put her own linen inside.

The next night, the farmer and his wife were able to sleep in their lovely new bedroom. The farmer's wife felt very pleased with herself as she snuggled down under the covers.

At midnight she awoke. The room was freezing! She and her husband looked at each other in the darkness as their teeth chattered. With a sudden rush of even colder air, their bedclothes were ripped away and the linen set to dancing!

That was just the beginning. In the kitchen, the milk was spilled and the flour bags were bust. At dinnertime, food and drink and plates and cups went flying.

These two weren't as hardy as the previous couple. It was only a few days later that they called for the parson.

The new young parson had been briefed by his predecessor about the ghost. He told the tale to the new owners.

'The old man was a fool, in my opinion,' he went on. 'Laying the ghost in a cupboard, of all places! It's a recipe for disaster.'

But when he came to exorcise it the ghost really didn't want to go. Long did the new parson cajole and plead, begging the ghost to move on. But it wouldn't. So round and round the house they went. Out of the bedroom and down the stairs he chased it, crucifix clutched in one hand, Bible in the other, the rugs and the curtains whipped about by the spirit. Into the kitchen, and the flour rose in a white mist. Out into the hall – and finally he bullied the spirit into the parlour.

Sweat pouring down his face, the parson repeated the prayers over and over as the ghost writhed and struggled. It banged open the door of the grandfather clock – and there the parson had it. He laid it into the pendulum, then called the farmer.

The farmer grabbed the pendulum and raced outside.

'Into the old well!' cried his wife, hauling up the cover.

Down it went with a splash, and the farmer slammed the lid back down.

The farmer and his wife had only daughters. When the farm came to be passed on, it was to the eldest daughter and her husband. The daughter loved the grandfather clock. She'd only been small when the ghost was laid, but she still remembered its comforting tick.

She'd often looked at it and sigh, 'Oh, how I wish that that old clock was working again.'

She never told her husband why the clock didn't work. Best not to trouble him with things like that. Like enough he'd not believe a word of it!

The husband doted on his wife and would do anything to please her. He decided to get the old clock working – as a surprise. He checked inside and ascertained that it had no pendulum. That was easy enough to fix – if he could just find it.

He asked around for its whereabouts, but no one seemed to know, even old hands who'd been on the farm for years. But he persisted. There was something about the way those old farmhands spoke that he didn't trust. At length, one of the old boys cracked and told him where to look … but he didn't tell him why it was there.

The farmer thought it a ridiculous tale, but when he lifted up the cover of the dry old well and looked down, there it was. He lowered a hook to hoick the pendulum up. It was freezing cold in his hands. Shaking his head once more at the strangeness of his late in-laws, he took it to his workshop and got the thing nicely shined up.

By the time his wife came home from market the pendulum was installed, the clock was wound and ticking and he was ready with his surprise.

But the surprise was on him.

When they sat down to dinner, they didn't get to take one bite of food before up went the potatoes, the plates, the knives and all! And down came the ale on the farmer's head.

His wife cried, 'What have you done?'

That night was a night of terror. The milk went flying, flour billowed through the air, the pendulum smashed back and forth in the clock and up in the best bedroom the bedclothes whipped off. The couple shivered till dawn in their nightshirts.

First thing, the farmer ran down to the church.

With the pendulum lying on the parlour table between them, the farmer's wife stuttered out her tale of haunts and devilry. 'Please, Reverend, can't you just lay this ghost once and for all?'

The new young parson shook his head. 'This may be too much for me, if neither of my predecessors could do it. But I might just know a way.'

A few days of spilt milk and tears later, the parson arrived with eleven of his colleagues.

Round the house they tracked the ghost until there was nowhere left for it to run. Back into the pendulum they trapped it. They begged, they pleaded, but still the spirit wouldn't go to his eternal rest, so out to the well they trooped and dropped the pendulum down once more.

The young farmer sealed up the well, and to make sure no one ever released the spirit again he built a pretty summerhouse for his wife over the top.

For years that family lived in the house and they had no more trouble from the ghost. But things change. These days, old farmhouses are desirable residences away from the hurly-burly of city life. These days, incomers outnumber village folk so much that in many places the old stories are forgotten. Not only that, but those incomers, they will change things – an extension here, a barn conversion there. Someday, someone's going to look at that old summerhouse and think, 'I could do better than that,' and once more the beer will go flying and once more a couple will wake in the night to find their bedroom freezing cold and their bedclothes thrown on to the floor!

26

The Vagabond Nun

As Prioress Katherine lay on her bed each breath was a rasp of pain. She didn't need the infirmarian to tell her there would be no way back from this. Part of her mind accepted that this was her deathbed and went through the motions of praying, but another part was panicking. She wasn't ready. She was only thirty-five. But it wasn't exactly that that frightened her. In the end, everyone must die, and she, the prioress of prosperous Bungay Priory, should have nothing to fear. She knew the younger nuns would be astonished to think that their busy, devout abbess should fear God's judgement, but the older ones who remembered what she'd done … they would understand.

Katherine closed her eyes and remembered …

She could still conjure the exact feeling of the rough, damp wool of her borrowed dress against her skin, and her cold cheeks slaked with rain as she stood on the path. She could still taste the bitter pill of despair as she waited, counting hour after hour for her cousin's men to come. Two nights out alone. Hard to believe that that was all it had been. She'd lived a lifetime in those two nights.

Katherine had always been destined to be a nun. She'd grown up Katherine de Montacute, a Wiltshire landowner's daughter. When she was twelve she came to Suffolk, fostered by the Earl of Suffolk, William de Ufford. A fleeting smile touched her lips as she thought of her cousin Joan, his wife, and how happy she'd been at Framlingham with Joan and her children. A bittersweet happiness, knowing she'd never hold a child of her own, but never is hard to understand when you're twelve.

When Joan had taken her to Bungay to join the nuns, she'd whispered to her that if she didn't like it Katherine would always have a home with her. But she'd loved her new life, making friends with the other novices, showing off her skills as an embroiderer, lifting her fine voice to praise the Lord in the church. The only thing that had sounded a wrong note was the prioress. Katherine's lips tightened. Ellen de Becclesworth. Even now, it was hard to forgive her. From the very first, it had been impossible to please her. Katherine could see her thin, cross face creased with wrinkles, lips pursed, as she looked Katherine up and down.

'A de Montacute and kin to the de Uffords. I'm sure she will be an augmentation to the house.' Spoken as if she thought Katherine would be anything but.

At first, Katherine had managed to avoid the prioress's attention. She'd been happy to take her vows a year later.

Joan wrote frequently, but then a letter came that stopped Katherine's heart. In William's hand, not Joan's. She opened the letter with shaking hands. When she had finished reading the few spare lines, it fell on her lap as the tears splashed down. Joan was dead, the baby with her. After that everything seemed to go wrong. The prioress had a fall and never seemed quite the same afterwards, confusing the litany and stumbling over readings. It made her angrier, sharper. Katherine remembered her taunting voice when she caught her bragging over embroidery, or lazing outside in the sun. Then Alice, one of the novices who'd become a nun with her, died. A cut gone bad and she was snatched away.

Katherine's faith seemed to disappear overnight. Her prayers were wasted. Why had God taken such goodness from the world? Surely there was no God. And she was no fit nun. Hadn't the prioress pointed that out, time and again? In all her time in the priory she had not given a thought to the walls that encompassed her world, but now they closed in on her. She had to escape! The idea became all consuming. She turned to William de Ufford for help, not really thinking he would – to leave the priory would take her outside the law – but he was willing.

Only his men never came. She'd waited all night. No going back after that, so she'd walked away into that grey spring day, into the rain, towards Framlingham.

Katherine smiled bitterly to herself as she remembered. What a silly girl! Of course she could have gone back. Going back was the only option she'd had, if she'd but known.

The first hours were terror. She half-ran, half-walked, sure she'd be captured and dragged back, sure she'd stumble upon Rumburgh Priory as she headed south. By now, they must have heard she'd gone. But there was no one about in the insistent rain. By nightfall she came to Linstead Parva. Into the inn she went, under its crudely painted sign of a hunting hound. Terror that they'd know just by looking at her shook her voice down to a whisper, but once she'd huddled in a dark corner the bowl of stew she'd bought was the best thing she'd ever tasted. She didn't dare think; just spooned it down.

As she was finishing, the door flew open and a man came in, soaked.

'I bring news from the sheriff: a nun has absconded from Bungay, and she is travelling apostate from parish to parish, in secular dress, in peril of her soul, and to the manifest scandal of her said Order! She must be caught – report any sightings to the sheriff.'

Katherine froze. They meant her.

The man went on, listing all the men who would be coming after her.

She was sure they would seize her right away, and half-rose to flee. But nothing happened. The messenger was offered a drink. He drank it down in his dripping cloak and then was on his way.

As soon as she dared, she slipped out into the night, her heart racing as she listened for her pursuers. There was no sound, save the pattering of the rain. No wind stirred the branches. Panting, she hunched down in a ditch like a hare in her form. When she was sure no one was following, she ran on, kilting up her skirts and feeling the cold mud spatter her legs.

Once, blind in the darkness, she splashed into a stream. Her shriek filled the sky. She crouched in the water, feeling soft things moving around her legs. She could die out here. Men like those in the inn, all homespun clothes and big hands, would find her sodden body. A shudder ran through her. If she died … what then? She was apostate. She would … but she mustn't think that way. She crawled out of the brook and squeezed the worst of the water from her gown, then forced herself to run again.

Out of the darkness loomed a hall. She could see lights burning, so her tired feet took her away into the darkness. She slowed to a dull, sodden walk, shuddering with cold as she went. It had stopped raining by now. She could see across the open fields. The moon revealed a hill ahead, with a squat church tower. Her heart leapt. Re-kilting her skirts, she headed towards the hill.

Something large bounded out of a thicket of trees and landed just in front of her. She froze. It froze. In the moonlight she saw it was a roebuck, his short antlers jutting up as he stared at her, quivering and erect. The moonlight silvered his red coat so he shone. They gazed at each other for a long moment, and Katherine held her breath. Then his eyes flickered to the side and he was away, bounding across the field. She stayed a long time after that, dazed and smiling.

She trudged up the claggy clay path to the church's small arched oak door. It was locked. She tried again, and again, but it wouldn't budge. She sank to the ground beside the door, numb. Who would lock a little out-of-the-way church like this?

'Sanctuary,' she whispered.

Then she realised. It was locked to her. She was apostate. No church was open to her now. As soon as she left the priory precinct she'd become excommunicate. She was damned, and there was no salvation to be found.

Sudden tears burst from her, and her faith flickered in her breast. 'Oh Lord,' she sobbed, 'I haven't forsaken you, I swear it – I –'

But what could she say? She was a vagabond. She was guilty of pride and anger and ... many things. She saw all that she had done as a nun and she bowed her head in shame. She had been heedless, foolish. But – the old woman hated her. She couldn't go back. The earl *said* he could fix it, but where were his men?

She had never felt so alone. So without God.

She passed the night shivering and miserable beside the church door. As the night receded into the grey of dawn, she was on her way, heading south.

Katherine opened her eyes and gazed at the patterns of sunlight on the white painted wall of her chamber. The memories tumbled one after another. She'd trudged, feet aching, and hollow with hunger. Seen the peasants toiling in the fields, and hidden from them. A kind woman offered her a bite to eat and told her of her own son, another vagabond, escaping from his lord – Katherine's own cousin de Ufford. As she'd walked on, Katherine had thought of that young man, now making a living in Norwich, and felt him a kindred spirit.

She remembered her first glimpse of Framlingham's keep rising above the woods, and the road, so familiar, leading down to the town. Could still taste the relief, so great that it brought her to her knees.

Suddenly, she'd heard hoof beats behind her, the jangle of tack, and, horrifyingly, a man's voice: 'Lady Katherine!'

She turned and saw a posse of knights riding down on her. So close she'd been! Her legs burst into life.

Her chest heaving, lungs burning, legs like lead, she ran – but it was hopeless. No man could outrun a horse, and she, exhausted, encumbered with skirts, stood no chance. The horses surrounded her, huge and snorting, and she stared up at her captors.

Only as the leader dismounted did she register his tunic, the white emblazoned with three red lozenges.

'Lady Katherine … Sister? Thank the Lord we've found you! We searched and searched … You are safe now.'

They were the earl's men. She knew their faces, their names.

She fainted.

She was sure, now, that those two days and two nights out had given her the weakness in her lungs that was killing her. After them, she'd lain sick for many days. If she closed her eyes she could still see the visions of her delirium, wandering endlessly down country lanes, the rain that fell was Christ's blood, covering her with shame, and she wept bloody tears and begged God to see her, but all was dark and cold. She saw the peasants thin and hungry in their houses, counting out farthing after farthing for the fat lords, saw men with bows and arrows running through the land, saw her sisters turn from her over and over. She still had those dreams of salvation denied, even though she'd never wavered from her course in the nineteen years since then.

And the reason she'd run? The old prioress's hate? It turned out to be William de Ufford's doing. He'd been politicking, the fool, to get Katherine named as the next prioress. Her! A chit of a girl with a puffed-up sense of her own importance. De Becclesworth, no noblewoman, had felt threatened from the start, and the apoplexy they realised she'd suffered, later, when another one felled her, exacerbated her anger and fear. She'd suffered in Katherine's brief absence. They both had their crosses to bear from those two long days.

They'd taken her back, of course. De Ufford had said she could stay with him, but she could see in his eyes what she herself knew. There was no choice but to return. She had already brought shame to her family, but more than that, she saw her way clearly. The fever had wiped the slate clean, leaving only one purpose – to make good the ills she'd caused, and make better what she'd seen outside, as best she could. There was a period of penance, of bread and beans and prayer, of suspicion and judgement by her fellows, but that had only hardened her resolve.

In the end, they'd made her prioress. Just three years after she'd run. She tried to make her world fairer and more just. Ensuring the tithes were not too severe, the burdens of work not too great, and that no woman in her care should feel the desperation she had felt. Lord, she had tried. She pushed and pushed, and the work brought her great contentment, but at the back of her mind was always the question, had God truly forgiven her?

She watched the sunlight for a little longer. Each breath was an effort of will. Then her eyes closed and the light faded …

She stood at a crossroads, and there was light ahead, blazing. Behind her, darkness. She cowered, afraid, sure the darkness would take her. She was unable to move, to go forward or back.

After a while, the light faded and the darkness abated. She was back in her chamber, but it was changed … Another woman's possessions stood in place of hers. She looked down at herself and saw she was as insubstantial as dust motes caught in a sunbeam. She heard singing in the chapel, and a smile came to her face. She was safe. She was home. Just as she'd felt all those years before when they had brought her back to her cell after her time as a vagabond. Now there was no reason to leave again.

Sometimes, in the dawn light, she still walks in the ruins of her priory. Always in the daylight she walks, for there is a fear that holds her there, a fear of the dark, a fear that God's forgiveness will never come, that leaves her unable to pass on to whatever awaits on the other side.

27

The Luck of Hintlesham

It was a letter from his sister Cecil that brought Sir Richard Savage Lloyd back home to Hintlesham Hall. He spent the long, tiring journey from his constituency in Devon in tense agitation, but he forgot his weariness as he ran into the house and straight up the stairs.

When he reached his young son's bedroom he knew he was almost too late. The room reeked of sickness, and the little boy, dwarfed by the huge bed, was no longer the chubby-cheeked lad he'd left behind. He seemed a wraith, his tiny chest hardly moving. Richard strode to his side, but the boy didn't seem to know he was there.

Richard's wife was standing across the bed from him. His new young wife, her belly starting to swell with the coming child.

'What ails him? Where is his nursemaid? Where is the doctor?' The last question went unsaid: Why did you not send for me?

His wife paled. 'You are home early, sir. I was not expecting you so soon.'

He stared. She seemed to realise how those words condemned her, and hurried on: 'The boy would not eat, I tried to coax him. The maid was no help so I sent her away. I saw no need to send for the doctor. I'm sure he will rally now you are here.'

Richard searched her tense face. Was she telling the truth? No need for a doctor? Clearly there was need! Why was it Cecil and not his wife who had written?

There was the smallest whimper from the bed. Richard wheeled back to his son, and put his arms around him. Moments later, the child's feeble breaths stilled, as if he had only been waiting for his father to come. As he held the boy, the sheet covering him fell away, and Richard couldn't help but see the bruises on the thin little arms. Looking up, he saw his wife's cheeks flush.

In the following days, as the funeral was arranged, Richard could barely bring himself to speak to his wife. He hardly knew what to think, but he kept his thoughts to himself. His wife was pregnant. He must not risk the child within her in angry confrontations.

I only hope she is a better mother to her own infant than she was to my poor boy, he thought. She had tried to soothe him with thoughts of this coming child, as if it would replace his first son! His sister's suspicions of maltreatment loomed large in his mind. He read her letter over and again and prayed that she was wrong to think ill of his wife.

When the pitiful little coffin was committed to the earth, Richard decided that the child should have a more fitting commemoration. One that would not allow people to forget him or how he had died. He waited to act until his new son was born safe and healthy, and then he called in an artist to create a wax effigy of the lost child. This representation wasn't as these effigies usually were, however, showing the deceased as happy and healthy as they had been in life; it showed the boy as he had died, emaciated and bruised. Richard had the figure placed in a glass case on the north staircase, overlooking the exuberant carved vases sprouting flowers and fruit. It stood in an alcove in full view of the household. He told himself he was not punishing his wife, but he knew that every time she went up or down she would have to pass this gruesome reminder.

One evening when Richard was sitting quietly in his library, the door from the south stairs flew open. In ran Lady Lloyd in a state of hysteria.

'How can you do this to me?' she cried. 'I cannot bear it any longer. I demand that you have that awful thing removed. Why do you punish me like this?'

Richard regarded her calmly, but inside he was furious. The words came tumbling out.

'Because you are to blame. I left you with my son thinking you would love him as your own. I saw the bruises! Do not lie to me about what you have done. Your ill treatment of my son is unforgiveable. Cecil blames herself that she did not realise sooner how bad things were. I blame myself for trusting you.' He stood to face her. 'Let me be clear. While this family lives at Hintlesham the effigy will remain. I shall put it in writing. I swear that ill fortune shall befall this house if it is removed or damaged!'

Her face paled. She stepped back from him, then, with a cry, she ran from the room and back up the stairs to her chamber.

Lady Lloyd was never allowed to forget. She begged and begged Richard to reconsider, but he would not. Every time she saw the effigy, those terrible days played and replayed inside her head. She had not meant to harm the boy. She had wanted to be a good stepmother, but she had felt so sick, so tired, in the early days of her pregnancy. When the child became ill and would not eat she had panicked. One time, when he'd turned his face from his food yet again, she'd gripped his little arms and shaken him. The child had only got worse, and now there were dark bruises on his arms and his eyes were black and staring. Terrified, she dismissed the nurse, refused to call the doctor. When Cecil visited, she'd tried to conceal her agitation. At night, alone in bed, she'd sobbed to herself, 'I wish the child would die before Richard comes home.'

The weight of Richard's blame wearied her, and she almost wished he would cast her aside. At least she'd never have to see that effigy again! But Richard stayed close to home, devoting himself to his estate. Watching her.

There were two more children. If her husband thought little of her, he adored them. To the world they presented a contented front, but she saw the blame in his eyes, never diminishing, as the years went by.

The effigy remained on the staircase for more than a hundred years, although Richard's descendants covered it with a curtain. It became known as 'The Luck of Hintlesham'.

In the early 1900s, the Lloyd-Anstruthers were planning a ball. Colonel Robert and his wife, Gertrude, had inherited the Hall twenty-five years before, but had leased it out and lived elsewhere for a decade. Now they were back and ready to celebrate.

They knew the story of what lay behind the curtain on the stairs, but it was rarely spoken of. They'd instructed their tenants not to move it. After all, it was part of the family's history.

Mrs Green, the new housekeeper, was not happy about it.

'Can't understand why they keep it there, horrible thing,' she muttered to herself. 'Never mind the tittle-tattling in the servants' hall about how the house's luck will go if it's removed. Superstitious nonsense! The house will look just so for this ball and I won't have the guests getting upset because they've taken a peek.'

She summoned Wilf, the gardener's boy, and told him to take the case out to a shed. Wilf knew the stories, and he wasn't happy, but he did as he was told, glancing fearfully around as if he felt the luck flowing away as he did so.

On the night of the ball the house was full of music and laughter. The grand saloon had been cleared of furniture and carpets. Lamplight sparkled on the mirrors, the paintings and the panelled walls. Couples circled under the elegant high ceiling and guests drifted in and out of the dining room, or ambled along the hallway to the library.

As the band struck up and the dancers took their places for another two-step there was a shuddering underfoot. People glanced at each other but the band played on and the dance began. Almost immediately the shuddering happened again. It grew until the whole room was shaking. The gas lamps shivered, and then panes of glass in the tall windows began to shatter. With a deafening bang, the huge mirror opposite the fireplace cracked from top to bottom. Terrified guests surged out into the grounds. They clung together as the earth gave a last couple of quakes. The night calmed and stilled. Miraculously, no one was hurt, but everyone was – literally – shaken. Motor cars and carriages set out into the darkness. Robert and Gertrude sat up all night in fear of more calamity.

The next morning as Robert stood looking at the broken windows and damaged roof the gardener approached cap in hand.

'Beggin' your pardon, Colonel,' he said. 'Young Wilf hev just told me as how Mrs Green had him put the boy's statue in the outhouse afore the dance. I said to him that weren't right and he shouldn't hev what with old Sir Richard's curse an' all, if you get my meanin', sir. But he say Mrs Green say he ought and so he thought he'd better and so he did, sir.'

Robert stared at the man. 'You mean the "Luck"? Why ever did she do that? It's not been moved for nigh on a hundred and forty years! Bring it back in, Fosker. We can't have any more bad luck – or worse – falling on us.'

The waxen boy was hurriedly replaced in its alcove on the north stairs. But it was too late. The Luck had been taken from the house. A couple of years later Hintlesham Hall was on the market. It passed out of the Lloyd family for good.

Hintlesham Hall has changed hands many times since then. The sad little figure in the glass case is long gone, and the alcove where it sat is gone too. Hintlesham Hall's a smart hotel now. The staff – and some guests – will tell you that there's a little boy in the house, a mischievous sprite who sits on the beds and pulls pillows from under peoples' heads. The corridors ring with his childish laughter as if he's released from the sorrow of his waxen effigy.

His stepmother remains as well. Lady Lloyd carried her sense of guilt beyond the grave. She repeats her journey from bedroom to library nightly, still seeking the forgiveness that never came. If you listen carefully, you may just hear footsteps on the south stairs and the door to the library may open, pushed by an unseen hand.

28

Witch and Rabbit

Betty Petch and Josiah Lovett dwelt on the edges of Icklingham life. Josiah was a poacher who lived alone with just his dog, Jenny, for company, but he kept the village supplied with ducks from the Lark and rabbits from the warren up by Deadman's Grave. Betty's skill lay in herbs, and many's the time the village women crept round to Betty's house seeking cures for this or that. If Josiah's talent with traps was welcomed in the village, Betty was feared. They whispered she'd curse you as soon as look at you and could speak with the ghosts of the parish.

Josiah had no fear of anyone. He didn't fear ghosts and he certainly didn't fear old women.

He took delight in tormenting Betty. The old woman would sit outside her front door, watching the world go by, and as he passed he'd beckon her. When she'd tottled down the path, he'd wave a plump rabbit in her face, as if offering it to her, but when she tried to take it he'd snatch it away, laughing. She would mutter after him, but he didn't care. What could she do to him?

But after a time there did seem something awry with his luck. Once, there'd scarce be a night he didn't come back with a bulging bag, but lately that bag was empty as often as not. Indeed, there seemed far fewer rabbits on the warren than there had been.

When he mentioned this to the other local poachers, they shook their heads.

'Thas wholly wrong, bor,' he was told. 'Thas teeming wi' the critters.'

Off Josiah went to Deadman's Grave. There wasn't a rabbit in sight up there, and all his traps were empty. Puzzled, he stared out at the empty moonscape of grass and sand, until his dog Jenny let out a tiny yip.

Racing across the warren was a solitary rabbit. It was strangely pale against the scrubby grass, but Josiah paid that no mind. At his signal, Jenny hared after it. But the rabbit was faster.

Suddenly, Jenny froze, staring at something Josiah couldn't see. Her tail went between her legs, and she ran back to him to cower at his feet. The rabbit disappeared over the hummock of Deadman's Grave with a defiant flash of its white bobtail. No other rabbits were to be seen.

With a trembling Jenny by his side Josiah hiked over to the river and took a brace of sleeping ducks. When the sun came up, the strangeness of the night ebbed away, and the worm of mischief turned in Josiah's belly. His feet took him to Betty's cottage, and, with a grin, he offered her one of the ducks, then snatched it away as she reached out. As he laughed, though, he couldn't but notice that she wasn't reacting as she usually did. She was just standing there and staring wearily at him.

Deflated, he set off to the village to sell the duck to anyone who could pay. It was a meagre sum he got, so that night found him back

on the warren once more. He waited till late, in case the change of time should have an effect on the bunnies' movements.

No such luck. The warren was as deserted as the night before, his traps just as empty. He and Jenny settled down to wait. They heard the bell at All Saints' sound the quarter-hour before midnight, then, as if conjured by the bell, up popped a rabbit.

Josiah was sure it was the same one as last night, all pale and strange. It jinked and ran almost like a hare. But no matter how fast Jenny ran, she could not catch it. For a quarter of an hour they chased it, and then they heard the bells sound midnight.

Jenny stopped dead. Josiah followed her gaze, and there, up on Deadman's Grave, sat the rabbit. It was white in the moonlight and as still as a statue. Josiah was caught by its gaze, unable to move while the bells pealed. As the last note died away, he saw its eyes flash a sudden red. He felt himself released and, with a bound, the rabbit was away.

Josiah ran all the way home with Jenny hard at his heels.

For the next few nights he turned his activity to the river and brought back ducks until his customers were sick of the sight of them.

'Get us some juicy rabbits, Josiah! No more of these fatty old ducks!'

The warren was empty and still. That night he roved all over, hardly caring if he was seen by the gamekeepers if he got the satisfaction of bagging a rabbit. He heard All Saints' bell toll eleven, and heard the quarter- and half-hour bells sound. But when quarter to midnight rang, Jenny gave a yip, and there was the white rabbit!

Josiah was determined to bag it. For the next quarter of an hour he and Jenny raced over the warren until his feet carried him right up to the mound of the grave.

The midnight bells began to ring and once again Josiah found himself gazing into the burning red eyes of the white rabbit atop the mound. As he stared, Jenny started to whine. Behind the rabbit, mist began to coalesce, thickening with every peal of the bells …

With the final peal, there, spectral against the starlit sky, stood a horse and rider.

Back home, Josiah lay awake with Jenny pressed tight against him, his thoughts racing.

The dead man of Deadman's Grave! For years he'd been going up there, and in all that time there'd been nothing more scary than a couple of close shaves with the keepers, but now it was all demon rabbits and ghosts!

Everyone knew the story. How an accident had killed horse and rider, and how they'd buried the man up there on the warren, and how he roamed at night, angry he'd not got a Christian burial. Josiah's grandfather, a poacher too, had told him the truth of it – that it was a poacher's tale, to keep folks away at night and to allow the likes of them to nobble the rabbits in peace. Turns out Grandad was dead wrong!

As the night wore on, Josiah's thoughts turned over and over. In the early hours they delivered up Betty's weary face as he whisked away that duck. He sat bolt upright. That was the morning after the first time he'd seen the white rabbit! It was *her* – she was the rabbit! They said that witches turned into rabbits and hares, didn't they? Didn't they say old Betty was a witch? And everyone knew she could speak to ghosts …

By daybreak he'd convinced himself and was determined to put a stop to her shenanigans. He'd learnt at an early age that cold iron kept out witches, so he took a nail and placed it in his gun.

Out he went alone, and at quarter to midnight he saw the white rabbit. He let it run about a bit. Let it think it had him again.

Then he raised his gun, aiming for the critter's legs, and fired.

There was a terrible screaming from the rabbit. Josiah saw red splashed on its fur as it raced away. This time it ran from Deadman's Grave, not to it. As the midnight bells rang out it headed back to the village. Through a gap in the hedge by the church the rabbit fled. Josiah followed it across the churchyard and down to the road. He watched as it limped up the road towards, yes, Betty's house.

He was round there first thing the next morning. Betty wasn't sitting outside her door. For the first time, Josiah felt a qualm about what he'd done. What if? It didn't bear thinking about. Besides, if she was a witch, she deserved all she'd got.

He pushed open the door. Old Betty was sitting by the fire with her leg stretched out and covered with a blood-stained bandage.

Josiah went away triumphant, sure he'd solved his problem and put a witch out of action. But he was wrong. The rabbits never came out on the warren for him again, and he was forced to look elsewhere for his employment. He blamed Betty, and he told the story of her transformation to anyone who'd listen.

The story went round the village like wildfire. Everything they'd suspected was confirmed! The hole in the hedge was investigated, and everyone said it was a witch's path all right. They began to avoid that spot at night.

Things could have got very difficult for Betty, but the village women still needed her herbs and potions. In fact, the story won her more respect, and people came from far and near to buy her medicaments and view the witch. But it won her no friends. If the villagers had been wary before, they were hostile now. Betty no longer sat outside her house. She didn't want to see them make the sign against witchcraft as they passed by.

She died alone and lonely, and was not much mourned, save when medicines were needed.

The villagers expected that the witch's path would no longer be used, being as there was no witch. They were wrong. One night a few months after her death, a lad decided to try his luck at poaching on the warren, and to take the shortcut through the hole in the hedge.

It was just after dusk when he got there. The hedge was full of shadows, and, right in the gap, there stood Betty's ghostly figure – and at her feet sat a white rabbit, staring back at him with red glowing eyes.

29

The Honington Ghost

Tom Graves wasn't normally afraid of anything. As an RAF police officer, he often said that he'd seen it all, but there was something about the base at RAF Honington that got him going. It was the dogs. They went wild every time they were taken across a particular spot on patrol. First time, shortly after he'd arrived, he thought it was an intruder, but when he reported it everyone had just laughed and said, no, they always do that there – it's the ghost.

Tom liked history, and he was new to Suffolk, so he read up about the haunting. Turned out there was a hanged man buried under that very spot. Old maps confirmed it: Gibbet Covert, and the fields Gibbet Close and Gibbet Cover. They'd discovered the truth of those names back in 1936 when they'd been digging the land to create the airfield. They'd dug up a gibbet cage – with the skeleton still in it!

Tom went to Moyses Hall in Bury to see the cage. The fake skeleton there leered up at him with a skeleton's usual gaping grin, and he read the sad tale that had led the man to the hanging rope and the gibbet. He'd come across plenty of sad tales as a young police officer before he'd come into the RAF, twenty years ago, but this story depressed him.

That night, on his way back home, he stopped at the Fox Inn at Honington and ordered a pint. The landlord, with that sixth sense they all have, spotted that he was off colour.

'You all right?'

Tom sighed, and told the landlord where he'd been that day, and why, expecting that the man would laugh.

The landlord did laugh, but then he tipped the wink to the girl behind the bar with him.

'You're in charge, Kaz,' he said. 'I've got a story for this here gentleman.' He turned back to Tom. 'What you may not know is that the story began right here, in the Fox.'

It had been a pedlar passing through early that Sunday morning, 15 September 1793, who had brought the first news of it. He'd found a white cotton bonnet, none too clean, by the side of the road. Seeing that the landlady of the Fox, Mrs Pendle, was up cleaning after a busy Saturday night, he dropped it off with her, in case the owner should come by. The landlady accepted it, and pressed a couple of farthings into his hands.

Not long after, the forlorn figure of twelve-year-old Elizabeth Nichols from Fakenham came by searching for her seventeen-year-old sister Sarah, who hadn't come home last night. The child sported a fresh bruise on her face – a gift, no doubt, from her father.

'It was only dusk when Sarah set out, and it's only a couple of miles there and back,' whispered the girl.

'She was here last night,' said Mrs Pendle. 'Come to buy a poke of flour for that stepmother of yours. So I sold her that, and some darning needles, and then she was off. She was here scarce fifteen minutes!'

Sarah had been in low spirits. She was usually all smiles for the lads – you might say she was wayward – but last night her face had been drawn and her manner sullen. Something was up, and no mistake. They'd commented on it in the bar afterwards.

Mrs Pendle showed Elizabeth the bonnet and saw the girl's face pale.

This worried the landlady. The child looked more scared than was warranted by the thought of her sister spending the night with some swain in a hayloft. As her husband, William, was setting out to ride to Thetford that morning, she told him what had happened. He promised he'd keep an eye out.

He didn't have to go far. By the track up to Willow Hall he glimpsed something white. He peered gingerly into the ditch – then reeled back.

Lying there like a broken doll was a young woman. Her skirts were rucked up, and, O Lord God, her mouth was full of blood and flies. A second glance confirmed his wife's worry. It was Sarah Nichols.

Back to Honington he rode, and raised the alarm. Then he turned around again and rode, hell for leather, up the road to Fakenham. It was barely a mile between the two villages, and the Nichols' house was the first in the village, a mean little place of lump clay and whitewash.

John Nichols was a hedge carpenter, employed, like many were, on the Euston estate, and as surly a man as you could imagine. His second son, Nathan, was following him in his career but didn't have his father's brains. The two of them were outside the house when William Pendle came riding up to tell them the dreadful news.

'Dead! Dear Lord have mercy on me!' cried John. Nathan merely looked uncomfortable. Over and over John said the same words until William was quite unnerved. The reaction in the house was no better. The girl's stepmother went back to making her dumplings. The other children sat stoically, but William could see that young Elizabeth had been crying.

Things moved fast. An inquest was called. Many stepped forward to say that John and Nathan were out that night. The murder weapon was found to be a hedge stake, a tool used by one of John's profession. The two men were arrested for Sarah's murder and carted off to Ipswich Gaol. In the villages people speculated why John and Nathan might have wanted to end Sarah's life. Her peakiness was commented on, and her sullen behaviour. It was easy to guess why she was peaky, they said, and would have become obvious with the passage of time. The only question: who was the father? In whispers people said it was surely her father or her brother.

In gaol, Nathan confessed to his sister's murder. It hadn't been his idea. His father had promised him a new pocket watch if he did the deed. He'd beaten his sister to death, then placed her garter around her neck to make it look like she'd strangled herself. He never gave the reason why John wanted her dead.

They were hanged at Bury on 26 March 1794. The son's body was given to medical science for dissection. John Nichols was brought home and his body gibbeted in a covert on the lane to Rymer Point on the Barnham Road.

Tom stared gloomily into his drink. 'Things never change. There are some that say capital punishment should come back – as a deterrent – but I say, look at cases like that. They knew the penalty for murder, yet they did it anyway. That poor girl. And then that gibbeted man he starts his haunting, does he?'

'Ah well,' said the landlord. 'It's a bit more complex than that …'

After the body was put up by the covert, no one liked to walk past the creaking cage with its bird-pecked remains, especially after dark, and people started to say that John Nichols was walking. Theories abounded, some saying he walked because he was guilty, some because he was innocent. Whatever the truth of it, a shadowy dark figure was seen in the trees. William Pendle heard much of that ghostly gossip in the Fox, so, when he heard two of his regulars talking that night, his ears pricked up.

'Thas just a corpse, when all's said and done,' said Percy Gathercole.

'No, no, no, that walks all right,' cried James Simper. 'My brother-in-law's apprentice's cousin that works up by Willow Hall he see'd it go by! He tole me, just a week ago it was, right here in the Fox!'

Percy just laughed.

'Well, then,' said James, a twinkle in his eye. 'You talk bold, but I'll wager you won't go up there and ask that ol' Nichols how he dew feel!'

But Percy had a fund of ale-fuelled courage and in a flash a sum was agreed and the two were shaking on it. William couldn't help notice that as soon as Percy was gone, James was out the door as well.

Percy walked briskly along, whistling as he went, up the road to the turn-off to the gibbet. Taylor's Grove sat dark on the hill above him. His whistling sputtered to a halt and, more hesitantly, he made his way along the track and on to the rough ground of Larkhall Heath. The moon was only quarter full, casting barely a sliver of light. The gorse and trees loomed large as Percy passed them. The hooting of an owl close by did little to settle his nerves. A rustling in the bushes hurried him on.

He saw the dark wedge of the covert ahead and, just ahead of it, the dark man-shape of the gibbet cage, swaying slightly – even though there was no breeze. He forced himself closer, until by the moonlight he could make out the bars of the cage and the rattling skeleton within. It looked just like it was grinning, though it surely had nothing to grin about.

'Well, Naaber Nichols,' he quavered. 'How dew you fare?'

To his horror, a rough voice answered: 'Wet, cold and hungry. And sick of being here!'

Percy gave a squawk, turned about and fled across the fields. He didn't stop running until he came to Ixworth Thorpe and saw the Royal Oak.

He burst through the door and cried, 'John Nichols mayn't be walking – but I tell you he's talking!' Then he collapsed.

It was a red-faced James Simper who came round to Percy's house the next day.

'It was all just a joke,' he said, looking down at the drawn face of his friend. 'I raced ahead and was hiding in the thicket. You duzzy ol' fool, it was me you heard.'

That tempered the ghost-tellers for a time, but the stories persisted.

One winter's day some six years after the murder, an old lady from Fakenham was making her way back from Rymer House after assisting with the wedding clothes for the daughter of the house. She was a hale old dear, and she'd been looking forward to the walk home. But, what with one thing and another, it was getting on for dark by the time she set out.

She walked briskly in the last of the light across towards Gibbet Covert. The desiccated remains of Nichols were swinging in the gathering breeze, but she didn't look up. She didn't like the look of him at the best of times, and in the dusk she really didn't want to meet his eye. He was quiet enough that night, the only noise a wild croaking from the whirling rooks above the copse.

As she came up to Larkhall Heath, she was sure she heard something behind her. A rustling noise, as if there was something in the hedge.

'Just the wind,' she told herself. 'Thas getting up a blow tonight.'

But once she was on the heath, though the rooks were now silent in the darkness of sleep, the rustling didn't stop. She was sure, in fact, that something was right behind her. Something breathing heavily. She whirled around, but there was nothing save the darkening hulks of gorse.

Taking a deep breath, on she went, but at once she heard a little patting sound on the springy earth. Footsteps? And that sighing, soughing sound. It sounded for all the world like … something dead drawing breath from a dried-out neck. She looked around once more, and as she stopped, so the patting noise stopped too, but in the gathering gloom there was nothing to be seen.

She quickened her step so her own breath heaved, but still behind her it came, matching pace for pace, that same tapping sound. Sure

now that ghostly feet were following, she sped out on to the path to Taylor's Covert.

The wood was dark, the heavy breathing seemed right by her ear, but no way could she go any faster. Still, she was through fast enough. There ahead she could see the road. She blessed the sight of it. Less than a mile till she was home!

As she stepped on to the road she heard the tapping sound once more, and although she knew it was a mistake, she turned around – and there, on the path behind her, stood a monster! Huge it was, and dark, and its hooves clip-clopped as it pressed towards her.

Nichols was become a cloven-hooved devil! Despite her aching bones, she broke into a run the speed of which would have pleased her in her youth.

The clop of hooves followed her, but she was able, just, to stay ahead. Here was her house. She burst through the gate, flung herself up the path and at the door.

'A monster!' she shrieked.

Her husband and daughter, hearing her cry, raced to the door with lanterns in their hands. The old lady lay in a faint on the step. In shock they raised their lanterns up. Staring back at them by the gate stood the fearful creature. The husband gathered up his wife and bore her inside, but the daughter turned back to the creature and held out her hand. The creature was all atremble. It shied as she approached, but with a handful of oats it was lured inside.

When the old woman awoke, she was confronted straight away by her terrible foe: a little donkey foal.

'He followed you home, you silly old besom!' cried her husband.

The old woman stared into the creature's dark doe eyes and laughed. 'We shall have to keep him!' The foal came forward and nuzzled at her hand. 'I shall call him Ghost!'

Tom laughed as the landlord finished his tale. 'So there never was any ghost, then? That makes no sense! The dogs go mad there; I'm sure there is something in it. Even in the daytime they won't go near.'

The landlord shrugged.

'I don't doubt you. Well, you know as they buried the skeleton right there back in '36, in the very spot they'd found him in his cage. Maybe it's just that dogs are more sensitive than us humans to things of the spirit – or maybe it was that disturbance made Nichols restless after so long asleep. Maybe taking his cage away didn't please him, and if that's so, you'll just have to get used to it, because I know that you'll never get that cage out of the museum now it's gone in!'

30

The Afterlife of St Edmund

For the blind man the setting of the sun made little difference, but he knew they couldn't go on any longer unless the boy's eyes could see.

'Come, lad. There's a village near, isn't there? I can smell cooking and hear voices. Shall we see if one of these homes will give charity to an old pilgrim and his boy? We can travel on to North Elmham tomorrow.'

When the people of Hoxne saw the poverty of the pilgrims, they turned them away. The old man and the boy were resigning themselves to another night curled in their cloaks by the wayside when the boy remembered passing a small tumbledown building close to the wood on the edge of the village.

The door to the shack was open. In they went and settled down for the night. Just as he drifted into sleep the boy thought he heard a wolf's howl, but sleep was too close and claimed him.

He awoke to light. At first he thought it was morning, but the light came from within the little building.

'It's a church,' he breathed, as he took in the altar, the lanterns, the glint of broken coloured glass in the tiny east window, the carved wooden – shrine?

His master was already praying by it. He turned to the boy. There were tears pouring down his cheeks. 'I can see. My child, I am healed!'

The boy stared at him in wonder and mumbled a prayer of thanks. But the light pouring from the shrine filled him with fear. 'What is this place, master?'

The old man beckoned him closer. The shrine was old and its paint peeling, but you could see it was intricately carved with a cross and —

'A wolf and a head? I don't understand.'

'I believe this is the shrine of St Edmund, who died a martyr's death fighting the Danes more than a hundred years ago. His severed head was protected by a wolf.'

At last the full import of his master's healing struck the boy.

'Master, this is a miracle! We must tell the world!'

Miracles came thick and fast once the site was rediscovered. In the early tenth century, the saint's body was moved to a place that soon gained the name Bury St Edmunds. There, the saint was guarded by a community of priests who devoted their lives to him. This new home must have pleased the saint, for the healing miracles continued. His church became a place of sanctuary.

One May Day nearly a hundred years after the saint came to Bury, Sheriff Leofstan was holding his court on Thingoe Hill, the meeting place of the hundred. Among those to be tried was Wulfswith, whose neighbours had accused her of stealing. She pleaded her innocence, but no one came forward to speak for her. She was found guilty.

In the hustle and bustle, Wulfswith was left alone for a moment. While her guards were busy with another captive, she seized her chance. Heart pounding, she fled down the hill and across the fields to the town. It was less than a mile, but her chest was soon heaving with the effort. When she reached the road, she tried not to run too fast or look too guilty. The wooden towers of St Edmund's church rising up above the houses gave her hope. She prayed that the saint would welcome her.

Gasping, 'Sanctuary!' she raced past the young priest on the gate and flung herself through the doors of the church. She collapsed in front of the jewel-crusted shrine and reached out a hand to clasp it. A faint glow rose up from the shrine and enveloped her. The priest on duty in the church, seeing the woman's dash to the shrine and the glow that followed, came and asked her what had happened. When he'd heard her story, he ran to the gate and whispered the tale in the ear of the priest guarding it.

Back on Thingoe Hill, Leofstan had realised what had happened. Furious, he ordered his men down into the town to find Wulfswith.

When they reached the gate of the church the young priest stood to bar their way. 'She has claimed sanctuary of St Edmund and the saint has accepted her.'

The men reported this to Leofstan with some trepidation.

The Sheriff's fury exploded. 'Those lily-livered priests have no jurisdiction over the rule of law. Come! I'll show you how it's done!'

Down to the church they marched. Leofstan walked up to the priest on the gate.

'You denied my men entrance, boy, but you will not deny me. That woman was tried in a court of law and found guilty. That law extends right over your church – so go in there and bring her out.'

The priest stood his ground. 'Once sanctuary has been given, my lord, it cannot be revoked. The saint himself has accepted her.'

Leofstan barked to his men to go in and seize the woman, but they hung back with fear on their faces.

'What? Afraid of a parcel of priests? I will fetch her myself!'

Knocking the young priest aside, he strode through the gate, drawing his sword as he went.

The woman was cowering by the shrine, a dirty lump of brown homespun against the glittering gold and jewels. He heard her gasp with fear. Then, suddenly, he was seized by agony so intense it brought him to his knees. His sword clanged on the marble floor.

Wulfswith watched as he writhed and howled on the floor, his face a mask of pain.

To the priest who'd helped her, she cried, 'You must help him!'

The priest shook his head. 'As this man has delivered judgement on many, so the saint has judged him and punishes him. It would go against the will of God to thwart the saint's will.'

Leofstan died screaming on the church floor. No one comforted him. When his body was offered to his guards to take away, they fled. The priests refused to bury him in consecrated ground. That night they carried him to Babwell Fen and dropped him in.

In the weeks that followed, Leofstan's lonely ghost was reported to be haunting the waterways, its mouth open in a silent wail of pain.

The new sheriff, keenly aware of his predecessor's fate, pardoned Wulfswith. 'The saint protects the just,' he said. 'Let him be a strong protector for our town. Let no one stand in his way!'

But only a few years later the town was in danger. Edmund's old enemies, the Danes, invaded England once more and East Anglia was laid waste. The Danes' leader, Sweyn Forkbeard, desired the wealth in St Edmund's rich shrine. People flocked to the shrine to beg the saint to intercede for them to stop the Danes.

But they seemed unstoppable. In 1010, at the Battle of Ringmere, near Thetford, they killed the flower of the East Anglian nobility and put the rest to flight. Elated with victory, Sweyn swore he'd subjugate England and take the land as his own.

That night Sweyn had a dark dream of a warrior king, who came in a blaze of glory with his sword drawn, and told him to leave England be. Sweyn knew who this warrior was, knew that St Edmund had reason to hate invading Danes, and he prepared to attack the town that sheltered the saint's relics.

The Church acted fast. The saint was spirited away to London for safekeeping. For three years Sweyn fought up and down the land, and for three years St Edmund lay in London. It seemed that the saint's warning had come to naught. Sweyn was crowned King of England on Christmas Day, 1013.

But the saint was just biding his time. On 3 February Sweyn was riding to an assembly in Lincolnshire when suddenly, right in front of him, appeared that same blazing warrior king.

'Help, my warriors!' cried Sweyn. 'St Edmund is come to kill me.'

No sooner did the words fall from his mouth than the saint swooped down on him. Sweyn clutched at his chest as if pierced by a sword. He fell from his horse, dead before he reached the ground.

It was his son, King Cnut, who learnt the lesson. Cnut replaced St Edmund's wooden church with a fine stone one and gave the monks lands and liberties. After he'd been wrested away from the London authorities, the saint settled into his new abbey, and the healings began once more.

Once, there came to Bury a woman with crippled legs. She could only drag herself around by the use of little stools she clutched in her hands. Each time she kissed the gilded shrine, she begged the saint, 'Please cure me. Please let it be me this time.' She swore to serve him with all the life she had left to her.

At each disappointment, she would drag herself back down to the west entrance where more hopeful pilgrims streamed through doors, and beg. When darkness fell and the candles were lit, the pilgrims would made their way back to the town's hostelries, but the old woman had nowhere to go. She'd curl herself into her threadbare cloak and huddle inside the church doors.

One night, Aelfweva, an Essex merchant's wife, was keeping vigil by the shrine. Kneeling on sore knees she saw light rising from the shrine. At first she thought a candle was flaring, but as the bright shining beacon of light swelled to fill the shrine she realised it was something else. A figure rose up from the shrine. He blazed with the same light and started to glide down through the choir stalls. Aelfweva was shaking in terror and wonder, but found the strength of will to follow him. The figure's brightness threw shadows of the huge piers across the church. It was as if the nave was bathed in summer sunlight.

The figure paused by the west doorway. There slept the old cripple woman. Aelfweva remembered pitying her and dropping a couple of coins in her hand as she'd come into the church. The golden figure smiled down on the old woman and sketched the sign of the cross over her. Then, ignoring Aelfweva, he turned and drifted back down the church, taking the light with him.

For a moment Aelfweva seethed with jealousy, then she hung her head. What pride she had, and what folly! No wonder the saint should bless an old beggar and not her. Just to see the saint was blessing enough. She shook her head and turned and was about to return to her vigil when she heard a cry.

She wheeled back, and in the dim candlelight she made out a figure standing by the door.

It was the old woman. Aelfweva ran over to her. There the woman stood as if she had never been lame in her life; tears streaming down her cheeks.

'I'm cured,' she whispered.

Aelfweva embraced the old woman and whispered in her ear what she had seen.

The old woman began to laugh. Before she knew it, Aelfweva was laughing too. The woman whirled her into a dance. Both laughing, both crying, they danced as the church bells began to ring for Matins. When the monks came in they stood and stared.

In 1182, when Abbot Samson began gathering together all the old stories of the saint's miracles, he came across Leofstan's tale among the many tales of healing. It horrified him, and out he went to Babwell to ask if the sheriff's lost soul still haunted the mere. The locals were only too happy to tell him the ghost was still there, its face still contorted in pain. Samson shook his head. It was time for this poor spirit to rest.

One misty, damp day, a waterman led Samson and his priests to a dark pool where no flowers bloomed and the reeds hung dank and brown.

As the priests began to pray, a thin white form emerged from the reeds, eyes hollow with pain and misery.

'Leofstan!' cried Samson. 'Do you repent? Do you recognise the rule of Jesus Christ?'

The spirit made no sound, but its mouth opened in a silent howl. Tears poured from the hollow eyes.

Samson pressed on: 'Do you consent to go to your judgement?'

As the face contorted again, Samson realised the ghost was afraid. Pity rose in him, for he knew this spirit might have good cause for fear. Despite his many years trapped in this desolate spot, many ages of purgatory would await him before he had atoned for his crimes. But better purgatory than being damned to this endless fear and pain.

The spirit twisted and turned about the mere, trying to escape the priests' prayers. Samson held the priests together until at last, with a final silent shriek, the spirit vanished. The sun burst through the clouds and the light sparkled on the water.

Samson ordered that a hospital be built in Babwell. To his mind, a place of healing and sanctuary was what was needed in a place so long haunted, that it in its turn should also find peace.

Still the saint kept watch for those who would harm his abbey. It was rumoured he had punished Prince Eustace, King Stephen's son. On returning in triumph to Cambridge Castle after stripping the abbey lands of their corn and goods, the first morsel that passed his lips struck him dead.

Edward I tried to threaten the abbey's privileges. That very night, he dreamt of Sweyn Forkbeard being slain by the warrior saint in his blazing robes. In the morning Edward withdrew his threat.

Henry VIII is said to have died with the words, 'the monks, the monks' on his lips, and there are those who say it was St Edmund who hastened him to his doom. But others say that when the monks realised that the writing was on the wall for their abbey they quietly took the body of St Edmund from its gold-encrusted tomb and carried it to their tranquil cemetery on the banks of the River Lark. With reverent prayers they laid the saint to rest, and there, they say, he has rested, quiet and at peace, ever since.

Bibliography

Anon., 'Ghostly Mansion Spotted in Suffolk' (*East Anglian Daily Times*, 10 October 2007)

Anon., *Hintlesham Hall: The House and its Associates* (Hintlesham Hall, n.d.)

Anon., *The Norfolk Wherry* (Norfolk Wherry Trust, 2012)

Arnold, T. (ed.), *Memorials of St Edmund's Abbey, Volume 1* (Her Majesty's Stationery Office, 1890)

Barker, H.R., *West Suffolk* (F.G. Pawsey, 1907)

Barrett-Jenkins, A., *A Selection of Ghost Stories, Smuggling Stories and Poems Connected with Southwold* (Southwold Press, 1986)

Beard, C., *Lucks and Talismans* (Sampson Lowe, 1934)

Becker, J. (ed.), *The Story of Southwold* (F. Jenkins, 1948)

Bradshaw, R., *Things That Go Bump at the Fort* (Landguard Fort Trust, 2009)

Brooke, J. & E., *Suffolk Prospect* (Country Book Club, 1965)

Brooks, P., *Suffolk Ghosts and Legends* (Halsgrove, 2009)

Bunn, I. (ed.), 'Mummified Cats!' (*Lantern*, 12, 1975–76, p. 9)

Bunn, I. (ed.), 'The Secret of "Kate's Parlour"' (*Lantern*, 28, 1979, p. 3)

Bunn, I. and H. Baker, *Haunted Lowestoft Revisited* (published by the authors with help from Lowestoft Heritage Workshop Centre, 2010)

Burgess, M., *Hidden East Anglia* (online)

Chamberlain, G., *Griffmonsters Great Walks* (online)

Cox, M. (ed.), *The Ghost Stories of M.R. James* (Tiger Books International, 1991)

Downes, W., *The Ghosts of Borley* (Wesley's Publications, 1993)

Dyson, B., *Great Livermere: A Parish with Ghosts* (Melrose Books, 2016)
Eaton, J., 'Through a Gate Darkly', *Memory Maps*, University of Essex, 2012 (online)
Evans, G.E. and D. Thompson, *The Leaping Hare* (Faber and Faber, 1972)
Farrer, E., *Yaxley Hall: Its Owners and Occupiers, Part 2* (Suffolk Institute of Archaeology and Natural History, 1918)
Forman, J., *Haunted East Anglia* (Robert Hale, 1974)
Gamlin, B., *Old Hall, East Bergholt: The History of a Suffolk Manor* (East Bergholt Society, 1995)
Geis, G. and I. Bunn, *A Trial of Witches* (Routledge, 1997)
Hare, S., *EeriePlace* (online)
Hippesley Coxe, A.D., *Haunted Britain* (Pan Books, 1975)
Jennings, P., *Haunted Suffolk* (Tempus, 2006)
Knott, S., *The Suffolk Churches Site* (online)
Lewes, M.L., *Stranger than Fiction* (William Rider, 1911)
Logan, F.D., *Runaway Religious in Medieval England, c. 1240–1540* (Cambridge University Press, 1996)
Mackinlay, Rev. J.B., *St Edmund, King and Martyr* (Art and Book Company, 1893)
Mackley, A., 'Short History of Blythburgh', *Blythweb*, 2001 (online)
Mills-West, H., *Ghosts of East Anglia* (Countryside Books, 1991)
Mower, M., *Foul Deeds and Suspicious Deaths in Suffolk* (Wharncliffe Books, 2008)
Murdie, A., *Haunted Bury St Edmunds* (Tempus, 2006)
Powell, E., *The Rising in East Anglia in 1381* (Cambridge University Press, 1896)
Puttick, B., *Ghosts of Suffolk* (Countryside Books, 1998)
Reeve, C., *Paranormal Suffolk* (Amberley, 2009)
Reynolds, D., *Just One More Smile* (CreateSpace, 2016)
Romer, C.J., 'The Vanishing House', 21 May 2000 (online)
Sampson, C., *The Ghosts of the Broads* (Jarrold, 1973)
Sanger, G.W., 'The Special Shrimp' (*East Anglian Magazine*, October 1961)

Siani, 'Rougham Mirage Ghost Mansion, Suffolk', *Strange Days*, 10 October 2007 (online)

Sones, B., *The Mermaid's Tale* (wpradio.co.uk, 2010)

Thompson, C.R., 'A Cunning Defence: The Coventry Act Conviction of Coke and Woodburne', *Dancing the Tyburn Jig: Crime and Punishment in 18th Century England*, 2014 (online)

Westwood, J. & J. Simpson, *Haunted England: The Penguin Book of Ghosts* (Penguin Books, 2008)

Westwood, J. & J. Simpson, *The Lore of the Land* (Penguin Books, 2006)

Index

3rd Battalion of the Bedfordshire Regiment 99, 103
63rd West Suffolk Regiment of Foot 34

Acton 27–8
Wimbrell Pond 27–9
Archer, Fred 122–6

Babwell Fen 193, 197
Beccles 11, 19, 46, 141–2, 146
Becclesworth, Ellen de 167
Blakemore, Anne 21–3, 25
Blois, Rev. Ralph 19–25
Blythburgh 104, 108
Blythburgh (Westwood) Lodge 104
Boadicea 27
Bradfield St George 39, 43
Bungay 166, 168
Bury St Edmunds 21–2, 32–7, 43, 48, 58, 61–2, 88–90, 92–3, 129, 183, 185,192–8
  Abbey 88–90, 92–3, 192–8
  Eastgate Street 33, 37
  Thingoe Hill 48, 192

Cambridge 58, 149, 197
Cambridge, John de 88–93
Cat 16, 49, 126–32
Cavendish 88
Cavendish, John de 88, 90, 93
Cavenham Heath 93
Clopton (nr Grundisburgh) 29
Clopton (nr Rattlesden) 29
Clopton Green 26, 29
Cullender, Rose 11, 45, 47–50

Dallinghoo 30
Dawson, Mathew 122–3
Denny, Amy 11, 45–50
Devil, the 18, 20, 42, 77
Dog 29, 179–82, 183, 189–90
Donkey 189
Dunwich 54, 135–6
Dunwich Heath 139

East Bergholt 38, 154–9
  Old Hall 154–9
Edmund, St 191–8
Edward I 197
Ely 90
Eustace, Prince 197

Fakenham Magna 184–5, 187
Felix, St 29

Felixstowe 98
Forkbeard, Sweyn 194
Framlingham 69, 166–7, 170
Freckenham 91
Freston 149–153

Gill, Tobias 11, 19–25
Goddard, Eliza 95–8
Goddard, Fred 97–8
Great Livermere 57–8
Great Yarmouth 46, 141–4

Halesworth, Thomas 89, 92
Harwich 99–100
Henry VIII 112, 198
Hintlesham Hall 173–7
Honington 183, 185
Horse 11, 16, 23, 48, 88, 93, 95, 101, 118, 133, 138–9
Hoxne 191–2
Hulver Street 133–4, 138
Hurr, William 13–8

Icklingham 87, 93, 178–82
  Deadman's Grave 180–1
Icknield Way 125
Ingworth, Dr Richard 113–4
Inkerman, Battle of 34
Ipswich 21–2, 39, 69, 106, 110–5, 148, 150–2, 185
  Buttermarket, The 111–5
  Cowells 110–1

James, Duke of York 51, 53
Jay's Hill, Sotterley 133, 138
Johnson, William 83

Kentford 123, 125
Kentwell Hall 69–74
King's Shropshire Light Infantry 154

Lakenheath 90
Lark, River 87, 92–3, 178, 198
Landguard Fort 99–104
Leeke, Francis 82–4, 86
Leeke, Margaret 82–3
Leeke, Nicholas 82–3
Leeke, Seymour 82–3, 86
Leofstan, Sheriff 11, 192–4, 197
Letheringham 75, 77
Lloyd, Sir Richard Savage 173–6
Long Melford 27–8, 88
Lowestoft 11, 44–5, 48, 50, 52, 117, 121, 133, 145
  Mariner's Street (Swan Lane) 47, 49–50
  Wilde's Score 44, 47, 49–50

May, Sam 13–4, 17
May, Jim 13–4
Mildenhall 90, 92–3
Montacute, Katherine de 166–172
Montagu, Edward, Earl of Sandwich 51–6

Nelson, Henrietta 81–6
Newmarket 91–2, 122–5
  Pegasus Stables 123–4
Nichols, Elizabeth 184–5
Nichols, John 185–7
Nichols, Nathan 185
Nichols, Sarah 185–6

Orford 30–1
Orwell, River 99, 148, 150, 152–3

Oulton Broad 140
Oulton High House 117–121

Pakenham 160–5
Potsford Wood 75–80

Rabbit 179–82
Rich, Sir Robert 19
Rougham 39–43

Samson, Abbot 197
Scotch Pearl 122–3
Snell, Jonah 75–80
Sole Bay 51, 56
Sotterley 133–5
Sotterley Hall 135, 138
Southwold 13–8, 22–3, 51–6
  Sutherland House (Cammells) 51–6
Spindler, George 94–8
Stoke (nr Ipswich) 152
Stour, River 99, 128
Sudbury 28, 127–32
  Mill Hotel, The 131

Thicknesse, Sir Philip 103

Ufford, William de 93, 166–7, 170–1

Walberswick 19–22, 25, 105
Westwood Marshes 105
Waveney, River 142, 146
Wenhaston 95–98
  Blackheath 95, 97
Westleton 94–5
Wherry Hotel, The 140–1
Wickhambrook 26–7
Wickham Market 77
Wickham St Paul 131
Wolsey, Thomas 148–9
Wrawe, John 88–9, 92

Yaxley Hall 81–6

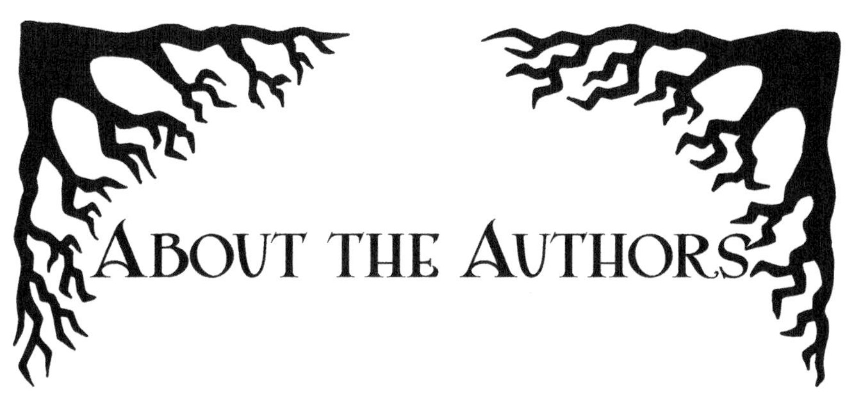

About the Authors

Kirsty Hartsiotis grew up in Suffolk, and has a deep love for the stories and the landscape of her home county. She has been a professional storyteller for over fifteen years and is the author of *Wiltshire Folk Tales*, *Suffolk Folk Tales* and *Gloucestershire Ghost Tales* (with Anthony Nanson). Kirsty is a member of the storytelling company Fire Springs, with whom she has co-produced many shows. Fascinated all her life by folklore and history, she has a special interest in telling stories for the heritage industry, in which she's worked for twenty years as a museum curator and educator.

Cherry Wilkinson has known Suffolk all her life and became a permanent resident in 1974. Educated at St Felix School in Southwold, she has lived in the south, centre and north of the county. Cherry grew up in a literary family and from an early age has been interested in local history, folklore and music. She has been a member of the Suffolk folk scene for many years, with a history of singing and playing that goes back to the 1970s. After a varied career in retail and horticulture her working life culminated in ten years of working for The National Trust.

If you enjoyed this book, you may also be interested in …

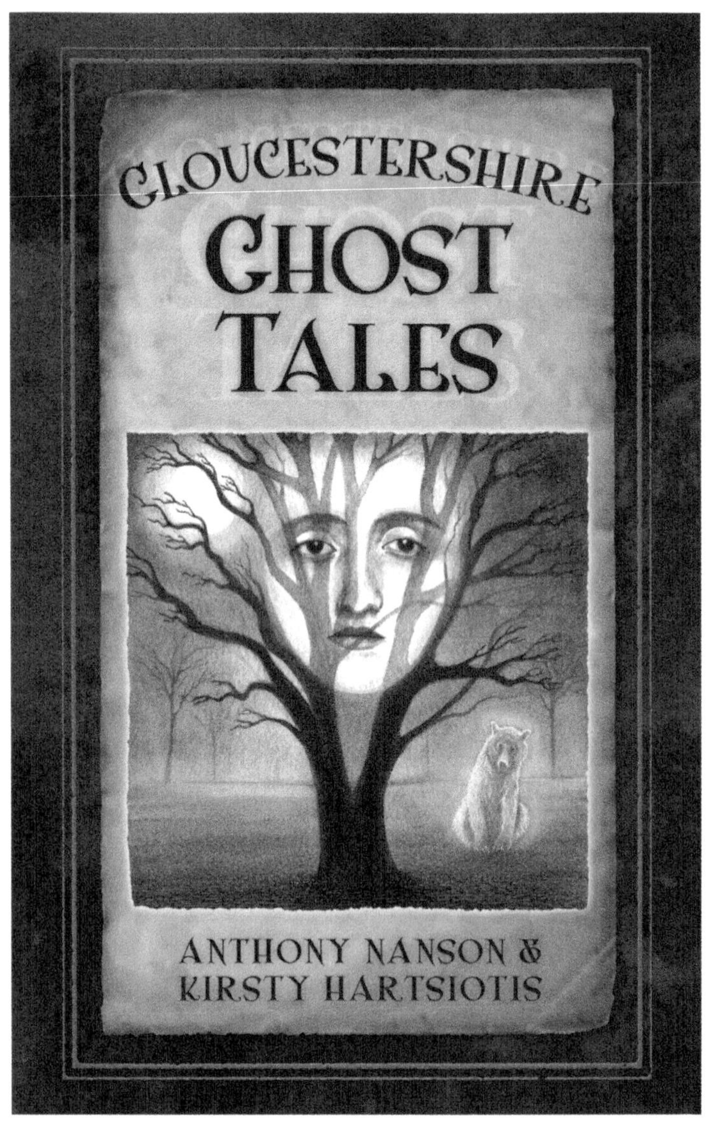

SUFFOLK FOLK TALES

KIRSTY HARTSIOTIS

Since 1993, the Society for Storytelling has championed the art of oral storytelling and the benefits it can provide – such as improving memory more than rote learning, promoting healing by stimulating the release of neuropeptides, or simply great entertainment! Storytellers, enthusiasts and academics support and are supported by this registered charity to ensure the art is nurtured and developed throughout the UK.

Many activities of the Society are available to all, such as locating storytellers on the Society website, taking part in our annual National Storytelling Week at the start of every February, purchasing our quarterly magazine *Storylines*, or attending our Annual Gathering – a chance to revel in engaging performances, inspiring workshops, and the company of like-minded people.

You can also become a member of the Society to support the work we do. In return, you receive free access to *Storylines*, discounted tickets to the Annual Gathering and other storytelling events, the opportunity to join our mentorship scheme for new storytellers, and more. Among our great deals for members is a 30% discount off titles in the *Folk Tales* series from The History Press website.

For more information, including how to join, please visit

www.sfs.org.uk